MW01146182

Anxiety Girl Series

Book 2

For Juliette; the bravest little girl I know.

THE HARDER YOU FALL.

THE STRONGER YOU RISE...

Chapter 1

Struggling to carry the final box up the garden path, I place it amongst the mountain of others and collapse into a heap on the couch. That's it. That is literally *everything* I own. Looking around the crowded living room, a quiver of excitement runs through my veins as I realise this is where I live now. This quaint cottage is actually my home. After six long months of dealing with estate agents and solicitors, I finally have the keys in my hand. Blossom View is officially mine.

Pulling over one of the cardboard boxes, I use it as a footstool and take in my new surroundings. The cream walls are littered with patchy squares from where photographs once hung and with a little elbow grease, the sash windows will be back to their best. Due to the age of the property, the ceilings are low and slightly wonky, with carvings from the many people who lived here before me etched into the woodwork. I strain my neck and try to decipher the faint lettering, fascinated by the thought of who put them there.

Letting out a happy sigh, I smile to myself and snuggle into the cushions. I knew from the moment I stepped over the threshold that I had to have this place. It just felt so right to me. With its thatched roof and wooden beams, it spoke to me in a way the dozens of other properties I viewed never did. I could almost hear the walls screaming my name as I soaked up its original character and charm. Yes, it's a little rough around the edges, but with a quick lick of paint here and there, Blossom View will be amazing.

My friends have made no secret of their reservations about this place and I can't say I blame them. They're of the firm opinion that a new job, a new pet and a new home is a lot to deal with so soon after an *episode*. No matter how hard I try to convince them that I'm ready for this, I can still see the concern in their eyes when they speak to me. The intense look of worry that overcomes them is impossible to disguise.

You see, just over six months ago, I went through a pretty rough time. The abrupt ending of my engagement marked the start of a very dark period in my life. I tried everything to move on and put the break-up behind me, but one unfortunate incident after the other made it excruciatingly difficult. My refusal to talk about how I was feeling led me down a frightening path that seemed impossible to get off. After a while, I started to believe the emptiness inside me was a normal feeling after the demise of a relationship. I assumed that the constant dread, which was eating away at my ability to function, was just part of the grieving process. It turns out, I was heading for a broken mind as well as a broken heart.

Looking back, panic attacks are what made me realise something was ultimately wrong. The paralysing fear that ran through my body at the onset of an attack is something I will never forget. Thankfully, with the help of my best friend, various self-help techniques and some much-needed counselling, I am finally feeling like myself again.

As strange as this may sound, I firmly believe that my experience with anxiety has made me a better person. My brush with mental illness changed my life in more ways than I could ever have imagined. Not only did it lead to my recent change in career, it gave me the keys to doors I never knew existed.

Before anxiety and depression came crashing into my life, I never really thought about matters of the mind. It's just not something you think about, is it? But since the day I was diagnosed, it has been at the forefront of my thoughts. For a short while, I was worried that I would never return to the person I was before and the truth is, I haven't. I *have* changed, but I have changed for the better. Although, it wasn't the anxiety that transformed me, it was the people I came into contact with at the support group.

If it wasn't for Anxiety Anonymous, I wouldn't have made it through that phase in my life. I wouldn't be here, in Blossom View. I wouldn't have taken the time to learn about myself and I certainly wouldn't have had the courage to alter the direction in which my life was going. My mind flits back to the day that I was offered the chance to become a counsellor and I marvel at how far I've come in such a short space of time.

Deciding to commit my life to helping others was a much bigger task than I anticipated. After months of training programmes, revision and educational courses, I finally started to realise just how much is involved with my new career choice. It might not be the easiest job I could have picked, but now that I've fallen into it, I wouldn't want to do anything else in the world. Through Anxiety Anonymous, I have met the most amazing people. People from all walks of life. People who are going through the same things I was going through and people who have taken the colossal step to reach out and ask for help. I still find it incredible to be on the other side of the circle. To be the one with the answers instead of the one with the questions is such an honourable position to be in.

Prior to my breakdown, my life looked so very different to how it does today. Sometimes, I walk down the lane to my old apartment and just reminisce about my time there. Everything from side-splitting laughter to gut-wrenching heartache took place in that beautiful building. Not surprisingly, once I had made the decision to sell, I had numerous buyers throwing offers at me left, right and centre. That's the beauty of living in Alderley Edge, property is always in high demand. The quick sale of my luxury apartment resulted in me staying with my best friend until I exchanged contracts on Blossom View.

As many of you know, Aldo and I lived together in the apartment for many years. However, now that he is cohabiting with his fiancé, Edward, the dynamics of our relationship have ever so slightly changed. Watching Aldo rustle up home-cooked meals of an evening was a rather pleasant surprise. Apart from the odd frozen pizza, during the entire time we lived together, I don't think I saw him use the oven once. A glass of fizz in one of Cheshire's many glitzy restaurants was more our style.

Despite Aldo's sudden growth in maturity, we're still as close as ever. In the past, I have referred to him as my rock, my support network and my spirit animal, all rolled into one beautiful, homosexual package.

Aldo Cristiano Taylor really is my favourite person on the planet.

When I was in the throes of anxiety, Aldo was the only one who dedicated his time and energy to helping me through it. Realising how alone you can feel when mentally suffering is the main reason I decided to ditch the artwork and become a counsellor. Knowing that I'm helping people on a daily basis gives my life purpose. It gives me a reason to dive out of bed in the morning and actually use my time to make a difference.

I've never believed in fate, destiny or anything else that was meant to be, but my roller coaster ride with anxiety has made me question my views. In less than a year, I've been through a mental breakdown, sold my apartment, became a counsellor and purchased a quaint cottage further down the lane. None of these were in my plans for the future, but as it turns out, I'm in the best position I have ever been in. I finally have a purpose, a path to follow and a goal to work towards.

Taking a deep breath, I look down at the keys in my hand and feel my lips stretch into a smile. If the past twelve months have taught me anything, it's that life is like a book. Every day is a new page, every month is a new chapter and every year is a new series. Some parts are better than others, but if you don't dust yourself down and keep on reading, you will never know just how good your story is yet to become...

Chapter 2

Gently stirring, I slowly peel open my eyes and look up at the strange ceiling above me. The realisation that I'm no longer in Aldo's spare room gives me a huge rush of adrenaline. Pushing myself up onto my elbows, I look around the bedroom and try to picture all of my belongings unpacked. Pulling the plush duvet up to my chin, I mentally remove the many cardboard boxes that are surrounding the bed. It's half the size of my old bedroom, but strangely, it seems to hold twice as much.

Instead of the open and almost clinical space I had grown accustomed to, this is cosy, unusual and seems to wrap its arms around you. The tiny stained-glass window casts a rainbow around the room, in an almost mythical way. I follow the array of colours that are dancing in the air and beam blissfully. It's as far away from my old place as it could possibly be, but it couldn't be more perfect if it tried. With a few subtle changes, I shall have this place looking like home in no time at all.

Allowing myself a final stretch, I throw back the sheets and feel around for my slippers. The old floorboards creak beneath my feet as I make my way through the sea of boxes to the bathroom. Releasing the latch, I wander over to the sink and stare at my reflection. Even through the dusty mirror, I can see that my face is alight with happiness. My green eyes pop against the paleness of my skin as I take a tissue and wipe the glass clean. The sparkle that was missing from my face has returned and I can actually enjoy looking at myself again.

Grabbing my toothbrush, I saunter around the room and make a mental list of everything that needs to be done to bring this place up to scratch. When I signed on the dotted line, I was so blinded by my love for the cottage that I didn't really put much thought into it. I convinced myself that a pot of paint and a new pair of curtains was all it required, but now that it's actually mine, I'm starting to see it in a new light. Maybe this is going to be a bigger job than I anticipated.

Not having the time to worry about it now, I quickly freshen up and head back into the bedroom. I have eight hours until I'm due to host the Anxiety Anonymous meeting and I intend to use them wisely. After quickly scouring through the many boxes for a pair of jeans, I throw open the curtains and gather my hair into a ponytail. Standing at the foot of the bed, I rest my hands on my hips and wonder where to start.

When I decided to sell the apartment, I had an almighty clear-out and left myself with what I thought were just the essentials, so I can't quite believe how much I have brought with me. From stacks of DVDs to piles of shoes and overflowing containers of bric-a-brac. It's amazing how much junk you can accumulate in twenty-six years.

Suddenly regretting my decision to not label the boxes, I pull the first one towards me and flip open the lid. Just as I'm tearing through a mountain of bubble wrap, there's a knock at the door. Squinting at my watch as I make my way down the stairs, I clap my hands together as I notice who's here.

'Hey!' I exclaim, pulling open the door and throwing my arms around Aldo's neck. 'Where is he? Where's Mateo?'

Rolling his eyes dramatically, Aldo reaches behind him and picks up a small crate. 'Don't worry! I didn't lose him. He's right here...'

Motioning for him to come inside, I take the crate and fiddle with the bolt. 'How's my favourite boy?' I sing, reaching inside and cradling the white ball of fluff.

'All those years of friendship to be replaced by a damn cat.' Aldo grumbles, shaking his head and leaning against the doorframe.

Flashing him a grin, I hold Mateo against my chest as he purrs happily. Delighted to be reunited with my little sidekick, I run my fingers through his coat as his piercing blue eyes narrow with glee. With yesterday being *moving day*, I asked Aldo to keep Mateo with him for the night whilst I settled in.

Just like me, Mateo has also been through a pretty hard time. After spending the first few years of his life at a rather lovely house in the village, Mateo was left to fend for himself when his owner suddenly passed away. Sadly, he wandered the streets for months before someone brought him into the local animal sanctuary.

It turns out, he was advertised in the local paper for weeks before I stumbled across the listing. The moment I saw his face staring back at me on the page, I just knew that he was meant for me. Aldo, on the other hand, wasn't so keen on the idea. Especially when he realised the pair of us would be staying with him for a little while. Despite his vocal protests, he secretly loves Mateo. I've noticed the odd smile and discreet stroke he gives him when he thinks no one is looking.

'How was he last night?' I ask, finally putting Mateo down and laughing as he immediately dances around my ankles.

'Loud. He meowed all night long.' Aldo shoots him a scowl and folds his arms. 'I thought you were unpacking?' He adds, casting a glance around the cluttered stairway and frowning.

'I made a start in the kitchen, but I must confess, I gave in to the lure of a glass of red early in the evening.' Motioning for him to follow me into the living room, I watch Mateo inquisitively investigate his new home. 'You can give me a hand in here, if you want?'

'Well, I didn't come over for a manicure...' Tugging off his leather jacket, Aldo carelessly tosses it onto the couch and tears open a box.

Smiling gratefully, I slip into the kitchen and quickly whip up a couple of frothy coffees. The sound of chirping birds floats in through the open window, filling the room with the beautiful noise of the countryside. Taking a moment to soak it up, I pop a few croissants onto a plate and head back into the living room.

'Where do you want these?' Aldo asks, holding up a selection of photographs.

Handing him a mug, I place the plate onto the coffee table and take the frames from him. A smile springs to my face as I run my eyes over the pictures.

Wearing silly sunglasses and giant sombreros, Aldo, Ruby and I clink our wine glasses together merrily. These were taken on my last day in the apartment. Just as I did for him, Aldo threw me a leaving party and it was the best day I've had in a very long time.

After our initial meeting at Anxiety Anonymous, Ruby and I gradually spent more and more time together and now, she's a firm fixture in our social group. It was actually Ruby who gave me the confidence to take the counselling job. When I first started the training courses, I questioned whether I was fit for the role, but Ruby was always on hand with a pep talk and reassuring hug to give me the confidence I needed to proceed. Looking down at the photographs, I feel a swell of pride as I realise just how much I have achieved with the help of my friends.

'How are you feeling?' Aldo asks, giving me the look that he always gives me when he asks that question.

'I'm fine...' Giving the pictures pride of place on the mantelpiece, I pick up my coffee and take a seat opposite him.

'Fine?' He repeats sceptically, plucking a croissant from the plate and taking a huge bite. 'Do you care to elaborate on that?'

Shaking my head in response, I choose not to reply. I know Aldo is only asking out of genuine concern for my well-being, but sometimes, his questions make me doubt myself. Surely I would know if I wasn't alright, wouldn't I?

Mateo jumps onto my knee and immediately curls up into a tiny ball. Regardless of how much others might question me, Mateo and I have this in the bag.

My biggest pet peeve with mental health, is that no matter how well you do later on in life, some people will never let you forget that you once had a breakdown. These days, I can't even cry at a sad movie without Aldo coming down on me like a ton of bricks. I pretend not to notice, but inside, it bothers me more than I allow people to know. I secretly worry that I'll never be allowed to fully put it behind me and close the door.

That's the beauty of Mateo. He doesn't ask any questions and I don't tell him any lies. He's just always there, always willing to listen and never judges. Nuzzling my nose against his, I feel my shoulders relax as he rhythmically purrs into my ear.

'How do you like your new home, Mateo?' I whisper, twirling his tail around my fingers. 'It's just you and me now...'

'Excuse me?' Aldo exclaims, putting down his mug with a thud. 'I think you will find *I* was here first.'

Letting out a giggle, I put Mateo on the floor and return to the unpacking.

'How's Edward?' I ask, busily filling the television cabinet with DVDs. 'Is he still enjoying his new job?'

'What do you think?' Aldo scoffs and proceeds to therapeutically pop the bubble wrap. 'He's like a pig in...'

'I thought as much.' I interject, before the air turns blue. 'I bet he's having a fabulous time out there.'

As Aldo proceeds to fill me in on how much fun Edward is having on his modelling assignment in Los Angeles, I unpack a box of coats and slip them onto hangers.

'When is he due back?' I ask, smoothing down my trusty parka jacket and collapsing the empty box.

'Six weeks.' Aldo murmurs, checking out his latest inking. 'At least I get some peace and quiet whilst he's gone.'

'You miss him really.' I tease, gathering the coats and piling them high.

He shrugs his shoulders and fills the chest of drawers with stacks of paperwork. 'Do you have work today?'

I nod and rip open yet another box. 'I'm chairing the Wilmslow meeting at eight.'

Aldo takes a glance at his watch and holds up a roll of paintbrushes. 'Where are these going?' He asks, turning them over in his hands and wiping a layer of dust from the top.

Glancing at the brush set, I feel my heart pang with longing. Since my encounter with anxiety, I simply haven't been able to paint. I've tried on many occasions, but each time results in me staring at a blank canvas for hours on end. It's as though someone has taken my artistic creativity and locked it in a box and it's a box that I can't fathom how to open.

'I'll put them upstairs.' Leaning across the coffee table, I take the brushes and stroke them fondly.

Squeezing past the boxes in the hallway, I jog up the stairs and push open the door to the spare room. I originally intended to make this my studio, but with my new job taking up the majority of my time and my artistic flair at an all-time low, I decided to dress it as a bedroom. Placing the roll on the dressing table, where my paint pots and canvases have already set up home, I take a seat on the bed and look out of the window.

As I watch the trees rustle against the side of the building, the door squeaks open to reveal a curious Mateo.

'*Meow...*' He purrs casually, turning his head from side to side as he pads into the room.

Stopping to inspect the new rug, he jumps up onto the bed and rolls around on the sheets. Not being able to resist joining in with him, I throw myself back and scratch his tummy playfully. I was a little worried about how Mateo would react to yet another change of address. In his few short years on this planet, he has been passed from pillar to post, but looking at him now, as he happily paws the duvet, I have a feeling we're going to be just fine...

Chapter 3

Adjusting the stand of pamphlets, I steal a glance at my watch and take a seat at the head of the circle. The meeting starts in just five minutes and the room is already starting to fill up. Raising my hand in acknowledgment to a couple of attendees I recognise, I clear my throat and get comfortable. Despite the many hours of training, it took me a little while to appreciate that every Anxiety Anonymous meeting is different. Different people, different problems and different requirements.

Hearing the clock strike eight, I wait for the room to fall into silence before speaking.

'Hi, everyone. Thank you for coming along this evening. For those of you who are joining us for the first time, my name is Sadie and I would like to welcome you to this Anxiety Anonymous meeting.' I pause for breath and smile easily at the dozen faces staring back at me. 'Regardless of where you are on your journey with anxiety, this meeting can help you get back on the path to mental wellness...'

I trail off as I hear the door squeak open behind me, effectively grabbing everyone's attention. Looking over my shoulder, I smile as a bearded man nods back at me and takes a seat at the far end of the room. Silently lowering his backpack to the floor, he pulls his brow into a frown and stares at me intently.

'Absolutely everything you say in this room is completely confidential.' I continue. 'You can share as much or as little as you like. There are no rules and there is no judgement.' I rest my hands in my lap and look around the room. 'So, does anyone have anything they would like to share with the group?'

There's a little hushed whispering, before a lady I recognise from previous meetings raises her hand.

'A few months ago, my husband started to have panic attacks.' She pushes her glasses up the bridge of her nose and exhales loudly. 'We came along to the support group a few times and I saw a massive improvement...'

I nod along and tuck my hair behind my ears, listening closely.

'For a while, he seemed to be back to his normal self, but he's slowly slipping back into his shell. It's like a cloud is constantly hanging over him and I don't know what to do to help.' Her voice wobbles and she covers her mouth with her hand.

'Unfortunately, it takes time and perseverance to conquer panic attacks and although it might seem impossible, they *can* be beaten. If you cast your mind back to the time where you saw an improvement in his disposition, was he doing anything differently?'

She nods enthusiastically and shuffles to the edge of her seat. 'He was using all the self-help practices and they helped him to actually talk about his feelings. The grounding technique proved to be particularly helpful when he had a panic attack, but now he is refusing to use it.'

Shaking her head, she pulls a tissue from the depths of her handbag and dabs at her glassy eyes.

'Sadly, many people will discover the profound effects of behavioural therapies, only to toss them aside once they see the results. As with many things in life, the mind takes time and commitment to see lasting changes.' I explain, making sure to include the rest of the group in the conversation. 'However, the positive side of this, is that you have seen just how effective these techniques can be. You have witnessed the success of these methods first-hand.'

Alec, a regular attendee, coughs and turns to face the crying lady. 'Is there a reason he isn't attending the meetings?'

'He feels like he's done with the meetings now. I've tried explaining to him that there isn't a quick-fix for what he's experiencing, but he refuses to dedicate any more time to this. In his eyes, attending these meetings is allowing the anxiety to interfere with his life.' The rest of the group nod in understanding as she speaks.

'I can relate to that.' Alec sighs loudly and crosses his legs. 'When my wife first suggested support groups, I dismissed the idea entirely. I'm not the kind of bloke who talks about his feelings easily. However, I've been attending Anxiety Anonymous for around a year now and I have seen a massive improvement...'

A small round of applause echoes around the group and Alec's cheeks flush violently.

'Thank you, but I'm not looking for recognition. The point I am making is that even after all this time, I *still* need a helping hand in dealing with my anxiety and that is nothing to be ashamed of.'

'Thank you for your input, Alec.' I smile gratefully at him and turn back to the room. 'I would like to add something to Alec's point. You don't have to attend the meetings in order to see long-term results, but you *do* have to keep up the techniques at home and that's where your husband has unfortunately taken a step back...'

Our latecomer coughs and I glance over in his direction. 'Is there anything you would like to add?' I ask softly, not wanting to put any pressure on him to speak.

Turning to look at me, he brings his dark eyes up to meet mine. Torment is etched onto his face, in a way that makes my heart pang with sadness. Slowly shaking his head, he looks down at the ground in silence.

Tearing my eyes away from the silent man, I lick my dry lips before addressing the room once more. 'I wish I could wave a magic wand and free you all from your mental demons, but the truth is, I can't. What I *can* do, is be a point of guidance and support in helping you all on your journey.' I pause and move my gaze from one person to the next, making sure to hold eye contact with everyone in the room. 'Anxiety can steal our thoughts, our sleep and even our inner peace, but together, we *can* and *will* take it back...'

Chapter 4

Clearing away the chairs, I leave the remaining people to chat amongst themselves and start to gather my belongings. As usual, a few members are making the most of the complimentary snacks and are sharing their stories over a coffee. Watching the scene in front of me, I notice our late arrival hovering by the information stand. Studying each flyer carefully, he squints at the writing before moving on to the next.

During my time with the support group, I've come across many men like this. Men who just need a gentle nudge to open up and take the next step by asking for help. At first, I was reluctant to approach people who seemed a little on the reserved side, but if experience has taught me anything, it's that initiating contact is almost always the best move.

Carefully making my way over to him, I tug my bag onto my shoulder and point at a glossy leaflet.

'This one I find particularly beneficial...' Reaching across the table, I take the pamphlet and hold it at arm's-length. 'There are lots of hints and tips in there on how to retrain the way you think. Plus, there's a great explanation of what exactly anxiety is.'

He stares at the leaflet for a moment too long, before reluctantly accepting it and folding the paper in half.

'Is this your first time with us?' I ask, leaning against the wall and offering him a friendly smile. 'I haven't noticed you here before.'

Nodding in response, he turns back to the stand of flyers and plucks a couple more from the display. His dark hair is peppered with grey, but something tells me he's much younger than he looks. Giving him a quick once-over, I notice his olive skin is littered with fine lines, like a map of the trauma that led him here.

'Well, my name is Sadie Valentine and I'm the counsellor here.' Holding out my hand for a polite shake, I'm taken aback by how deep his voice is when finally speaks.

'Aidan Wilder.' Accepting my hand, he shakes it firmly before folding his arms defensively.

I'm about to explain the whole point of Anxiety Anonymous is that you don't have to disclose any information about yourself, when Aidan picks up his backpack and heads for the exit. Watching the door close behind him, I exhale quietly and straighten the information stand. I meet people from all walks of life here at the support group, but every so often, I come across someone who intrigues me that little bit more. Of course, everyone comes here for the same reason, but Aidan has an air of immense torment surrounding him that is so overwhelmingly powerful, I can almost feel it myself.

Abandoning the pamphlets, I tug on my jacket and say goodbye to the few remaining people in the coffee area. Seeing them chat amongst themselves after the meetings is one of my favourite things about Anxiety Anonymous. People don't just come here to talk to me and listen to my words of wisdom, they come here to integrate with others who are just like them. They understand one another completely and that creates an open environment for them to feel comfortable in.

Anxiety Anonymous isn't just a support group, it's a huge part of people's lives.

With a final glance over my shoulder, I push my way outside and leave them to talk. The sun is starting to set in the distance, casting the world in beautiful shades of orange and red. Tipping back my head, I take a moment to study the clouds. I've always thought of the sky as a giant canvas, one which Mother Nature paints every evening and erases each morning. Just like you and me, she has good days and bad days. Some of her creations are better than others, but every display is uniquely beautiful.

Forcing myself to carry on walking, I slip my hands into my pockets and head towards Blossom View. With it being late spring, the air is slightly warm as it blows through my hair, causing strands of blonde to stick to my lip gloss. Picking up my pace, I weave between the clusters of people on the crowded pavement. Joyful chatter floats out of the many bars and restaurants that line the roadside, enticing you in for a glass of fizz, or two. Reminding myself that I still have unpacking to do, I carry on walking and breathe in the fresh air.

Spotting my old apartment block ahead, a plethora of emotions rush through my veins. It's like coming face-to-face with an ex. All of those old feelings come flooding back and you're powerless to stop them. Looking down at the ground, I give the familiar building a sideways glance. Even though I pass the apartment block that I used to call home multiple times a day, I still find it weirdly difficult to look at.

I know this sounds crazy, but I almost blame my previous address for my downfall. It's as though the apartment is where the old me still resides. The version of me that crumbled and allowed herself to be defeated by the darkness in her mind. Out here, I am strong. I am independent and I am free from the torment that poisoned my thoughts and killed my spirit.

Leaves rustle in the breeze, creating a soothing soundtrack as I pound my feet against the pavement. Tucking my hair behind my ears, I stop in my tracks as a Range Rover starts to reverse from the driveway to my left, completely blocking my path. Looking back at the apartment block as I wait for the car to leave, my eyes land on a shadowy figure sat at the bus stop. Squinting for a better view, I'm surprised to discover that it's Aidan from the support group. Keeping his eyes fixed on the ground, he rests his head in his hands, just like he did in the Anxiety Anonymous meeting.

As I look on, a bus fires down the lane, before coming to a steady stop in front of him. Slowly pushing himself to his feet, he steps on board without even looking at the destination. Nobody uses that bus route. Apart from the odd pensioner visiting family in the next village, it's usually completely vacant. Telling myself it's none of my business, I carry on walking until I reach Blossom View.

One of the most difficult things about being a counsellor, is that I find it extremely hard to accept my role finishes the moment I step out of the meeting. Just because I'm not being paid doesn't mean I can turn off my desire to help people. Ironically, it's like anxiety itself. It's not a switch you can flip *on* and *off* when the mood suits. Having been through the torment of anxiety myself, I understand more than anyone just how lonely it can make you feel. Anxiety and depression have a way of making you feel alone in a room filled with people. You can be surrounded by friends, family and acquaintances, yet still feel like you don't have anyone to turn to.

Trying to push all thoughts of Anxiety Anonymous to the back of my mind, I slip my key into the door.

'Hello!' I gush, as Mateo fires down the stairs to greet me. 'Have you made yourself at home today?'

'*Meow...*' He purrs, plucking at the rug with his claws and rubbing his head against my ankles.

Shaking off my jacket, I hang it on the coat stand and pop my head into the living room. Aldo and I did a mammoth job earlier and now, splashes of my personality are scattered around the place, breathing life back into the old cottage. My artwork hangs on the walls, photographs sit on the windowsill and my favourite crystal vase stands proudly on the coffee table. It's like I have finally arrived. This is it. Home sweet home.

Beaming in satisfaction, I wander into the kitchen and fill Mateo's bowl with food. Meowing happily, he immediately dives into his dinner. Turning my attention to my own grumbling stomach, I turn on the oven and pull open the fridge. Realising my options are limited, I plump for a baked potato and pop it into the oven.

Pushing open the back door, I step into the garden and take a seat on the iron bench, which was left here by the previous owners. The neighbour's apple tree hangs over the fence, resulting in a collection of vivid fruits falling into the grass at the bottom of the yard.

The garden was one of the main reasons I chose to buy this place. It's like a secluded little wonderland, bursting with life and the magic of all things green.

Allowing my eyes to close, I listen to the cherry blossom whisper as the wind whooshes through its branches. This year has given me a new-found love for spring. It's that one time of the year where new life starts to appear right before your eyes. Spring brings growth, it brings clarity and most importantly, it reminds us that it's time for something more beautiful...

Chapter 5

'Thanks for coming along today.' I smile at Ruby and link my arm through hers. 'I miss seeing you at the meetings.'

Grinning back at me as we walk along the leafy street, Ruby rests her head on my shoulder. 'I know, but I'm in a really good place. Not having to rely on the support group to get through the day anymore is a great feeling.'

After almost two years of regular visits to Anxiety Anonymous, Ruby has been panic-attack-free for five months and she's now starting a new chapter in her life. For so long, she allowed her anxiety to put the brakes on any plans that she dared to make, but looking at her now causes my heart swell with pride.

'How are you finding Escapism?' I ask, slipping on my sunglasses as the sun peeps out from behind a fluffy cloud.

Being so consumed with her mental health, Ruby never pursued her dreams to travel the world, but with a little encouragement, she took the giant step of joining the travel industry.

'I'm really enjoying it, but it's giving me a serious case of wanderlust.' Tucking her aubergine waves behind her ears, she smiles brightly. 'Booking people onto their dream holidays is amazing, but I spend all day fantasising about white sands and clear waters.'

'Where would *your* dream holiday destination be?' I interrupt, turning to face her. 'If you could go anywhere in the world, where would you go?'

Stopping in her tracks, she screws up her nose and looks deep in thought. 'Probably the Seychelles. They're quiet, tropical and the perfect escape from reality.'

'That sounds incredible.' We turn left and push open the gate to the park.

'Doesn't it just...' Ruby motions towards an empty bench across the field and I follow her lead.

The verdant park is practically deserted. Apart from a small exercise class in the tennis court, we are completely alone. Dumping my handbag onto the bench, I pull out the sandwiches we bought earlier and hand one to Ruby.

'How's the new place?' She asks, ripping open the box and taking a giant-sized bite. 'Have you unpacked?'

'Pretty much.' I tear off a chunk of bread and chew happily. 'Yesterday, Mateo and I spent all afternoon making trips to the recycling centre with cardboard boxes.'

'You took *Mateo* to the recycling centre?' She laughs, quickly polishing off her lunch. 'You're crazy.'

'That's me...' Wiping my hands on a napkin, I grab my phone and bring up my Twitter account. 'A crazy cat lady.'

'Speaking of crazies...' Ruby pauses and studies my face carefully. 'Aldo and I saw Piper in the village. She asked about you.'

My heart skips a beat and I try to hide my discomfort with a cough. Piper, along with Ivy and

Zara, are three girls I used to call my friends. When I was in the grips of anxiety, it soon became apparent that I was no longer on their radar.

'It's nice of her to ask, but I have no interest in building bridges with her.' Taking a swig of water, I slip my handset back into my bag.

'I can understand that.' Ruby nods along and bends down to pluck a daisy from the grass. 'Not everyone is meant to stay in your life forever. Sometimes, they're only there long enough to teach us a lesson...'

I stare up at the sky, allowing her words to sink in. Keeping friendships shouldn't be a chore. If someone wants to be a part of your life, they'll make an effort to be in it. I've always believed that when the going gets tough, you realise who your real friends are. There's no sense in reserving a place in your heart for people who don't want to stay.

'Has your mum paid a visit to Blossom View yet?' Ruby asks, tactfully trying to change the subject.

'She tagged along when I took some measurements last week. I was glad she made the effort, but she criticised absolutely everything and proceeded to tell me I was a fool for giving up the apartment...' My voice trails off as I recall the day I tried to impress my mother with my new home.

The disdain was clear to see the second her Bentley pulled up outside the cottage. Her lip curled up in contempt as I ecstatically showed her the old characteristics of the building, refusing to acknowledge anything I said with more than a swift nod of the head. My mother and I have never had a loving relationship, but I'm finally accepting that this is just the way things are between us.

'How's *your* mum?' I mumble, batting away an excited bumble bee. 'I seem to remember you mentioning it's her birthday soon?'

'It's tomorrow. We're throwing her a party on Saturday, if you and Aldo want to come along?' Ruby twirls a strand of hair around her finger and knocks some breadcrumbs off her lap. 'I should warn you though, it can get pretty crazy on the farm.'

'We would love to come.' I smile happily and clap my hands together. 'It will be great to put faces to the names I hear so much about!'

Frowning sceptically, Ruby shakes her head and stands to her feet. 'It's your funeral.'

Letting out a laugh, I dust myself down as we retrace our steps to the car park. Not having the perfect family myself, I completely understand Ruby's apprehension at introducing her friends to her nearest and dearest. Merging those two parts of your life for the first time is always a daunting experience.

'What are your plans for tonight?' She asks, letting out a yawn as we duck beneath the branches of an overgrown tree.

'I'm going to attempt some home cooking.' I announce proudly.

Spotting Ruby's jaw drop open, I shoot her a scowl.

'I'm serious! There's an apple tree at the end of the garden and I'm going to make a pie...'

Erupting into a fit of giggles, Ruby bats my arm playfully and shakes her head.

'Go ahead, laugh all you want, but the proof shall be in the pudding...'

Chapter 6

After several unsuccessful attempts at baking last night, I eventually gave up and resorted to ordering a pizza. It turns out, using a range cooker isn't as easy as it looks. Despite purchasing a cookery book and following the guidelines exactly, the results of two hours slaving in the kitchen were less than impressive. However, today is a new day and I intend to turn my hand to something else. I *will* become a domesticated goddess if it kills me.

Glancing at the clock on the wall, I suddenly realise Aldo should be here at any moment. Little does he know that he'll be joining me in a spot of gardening. With my only meeting of the day being in Wilmslow this evening, I have a whole day of sunshine to fill and I'm dragging Aldo along for the ride.

Polishing off my coffee, I dump the empty mug in the sink and gather my gardening paraphernalia on the counter. Due to the fact I've never had a garden of my own before, it's no secret that I don't really know what I'm doing. My last-minute dash around the garden centre last night resulted in me blindly throwing a variety of things into the shopping trolley. As a result, I returned with a selection of flower seeds, some scary-looking tools and a couple of pairs of gardening gloves.

Feeling rather optimistic, I pull on an old t-shirt as Aldo's voice echoes down the hallway.

'Shirley?'

'Are you ever going to drop that dratted nickname?' I mutter, reaching up and planting a pink kiss on his cheek.

Choosing to ignore me, he frowns at my tired choice of clothing. 'What the hell are you wearing?'

'Exactly what *you* shall be wearing...' Leaning across the table, I pull another t-shirt from the back of a chair. 'We're gardening!'

Aldo's eyes dart from the faded t-shirt to the shovel by the back door. 'I think I'll pass.'

'Oh, come on!' I protest, trying to wrestle him out of his leather jacket. 'Please?'

Rolling his eyes, he reluctantly takes the faded top and pulls it over his head, taking extra care not to disrupt his man-bun.

'Still not smoking?' I ask, spotting the nicotine patch on his bicep.

He grumbles something I don't care to repeat and follows me outside into the garden.

'*Meow...*' Mateo purrs, before rolling around on the grass playfully.

Quickly snapping a picture of him on my phone, I rest my hands on my hips and turn to face Aldo.

'What do I do with this thing?' He asks, weighing up a double-ended trowel dubiously.

Not wanting to admit that I don't have a clue what I'm doing, I pretend I haven't heard him and kneel down beside the flower bed. Quickly running my eyes over the instructions on a packet of seeds, I nod confidently and pass him a spade.

'We just need to turn over the soil, plant the seeds and that's pretty much it...' I tear open the box and ignore Aldo's cynical frown.

For a short while, we dig in a comfortable silence. The delicate sound of chirping birds in the trees overhead fills the air as we attack the soil with our implements.

'I'm really proud of you, Shirley.' Aldo says suddenly, wiping his brow on his forearm and sitting cross-legged on the grass. 'You've really turned your life around.'

Smiling back at him, I continue to dig until I reach fresh soil, not wanting to engage in the conversation.

'There's a small part of me that thinks I still need to keep an eye on you and make sure you don't slip back into, you know...'

As much as it pains me to hear Aldo talk about that time in my life, I completely understand his concerns. You don't forget discovering your best friend overdosed on the bathroom floor in a hurry. My training for the support group has taught me that anxiety can affect those closest to the sufferer just as much as the sufferer themselves.

'I wanted to run something past you...' Aldo muses, pulling off his gardening gloves to reveal a black manicure. 'How do you feel about getting back into the dating game?'

My blood runs cold and I bite my lip, not really knowing what to say. My last relationship was enough to put me off men for life. After all, my disastrous engagement was the trigger of my downward spiral in the first place.

'I don't know.' I mumble, watching Mateo bat a tulip and immediately run away. 'I haven't even thought about men for the past six months.'

'Well, I met someone at the salon who I think would be *perfect* for you.' He looks down at his nicotine patch and smooths down the crumpled corners. 'He owns an art gallery in Chester and lives right here in the village. He's funny, sophisticated and absolutely loves bloody cats.'

Aldo lets out a laugh and I can't help but return it.

'How would you feel about going for dinner with him?'

My heart wants to yell *no*, but my head warns me that the longer I leave it, the harder it will be to put myself out there again.

'It's just a bite to eat.' Aldo persists. 'I wouldn't ask if I wasn't one hundred percent sure you would love him.'

Not feeling ready to lower my guard and allow someone to get close to me again, I go with my heart and shake my head.

'To be honest, I think Mateo is the only man for me right now.' Sensing that we're talking about him, he pads down the path and curls up in a ball next to me.

Aldo studies my face intently, before reluctantly nodding in agreement. 'That's fair enough, but you don't need to decide right now. Just think about it.'

I respond with a swift nod and smile as he returns his attention to the flower bed. Tipping the seeds into the palm of my hand, I let them fall through my fingers and think about Aldo's proposition. If there was anyone in the world I would trust to pick a partner for me, it would be Aldo. I just find it hard to believe he knows what's best for me, when I don't even know myself...

Chapter 7

'People with post-traumatic stress disorder are often plagued with panic attacks, especially when subjected to people, places and activities that remind them of the trauma they have experienced.' Shuffling the stack of papers in my lap, I exhale slowly and look around the circle. 'As Jackson has just described, the fear and trepidation of a panic attack can bring a whole new dose of anxiety...'

Jackson sighs heavily and holds his head in his hands. 'I never used to be like this. Before my stint in the army, I was fun-loving, outgoing and the life and soul of every party. Now, I just sit in my flat, watching the world drift by and wondering if I'm ever going to be a part of it again. I'm just not *me* anymore.'

My heart pangs as I look into Jackson's brown eyes. Listening to people whilst they confide their torment in you doesn't get any easier. If anything, it gets harder with every story you hear and each tear that falls.

'I remember having that exact realisation. For any sufferer, the moment when you realise you're no longer yourself is monumental. Acknowledging that something is wrong is the first step in getting the help you need.' Pausing for breath, I bite my lip and shuffle to the edge of my seat. 'I appreciate this is your first time with us and you should be incredibly proud of yourself for making the decision to walk through that door today...'

Alec starts to clap and before long, the entire circle joins in with him.

'The road back to mental wellness isn't always quick or easy. However, with help and advice from myself and other members here at Anxiety Anonymous, you can rest assured that you will be guided every step of the way.'

The room erupts into applause once more, nicely concluding our meeting.

'I'm afraid we're out of time, but I would like to take this opportunity to thank you for joining us. I do hope to see you all on Monday. In the meantime, there's the Anxiety Anonymous forum if you find yourselves struggling over the weekend.'

One by one, people grab their possessions and start to make their way towards the door. Watching a couple of regular attendees hang back to chat over a biscuit, I flash them a smile and make my way down the lobby. Realising that the information stand needs replenishing, I grab a pen from my handbag and make a note of the flyers I need to order.

As I busily scribble down serial numbers, I hear the door squeak open and look up to see a dishevelled Aidan standing in the doorway.

Staring back at me in complete silence, his dark eyes burn into mine. His beard is even longer than it was at the last meeting, but the anguish on his face is just as raw as I remember it.

'Hi.' I mumble, offering him a welcoming smile as he fidgets with his sleeve nervously. 'I'm afraid you've missed the meeting.'

A dawning realisation creeps onto his face as he looks at the clock on the wall. Hanging his head, he rubs his temples and lets out an exhausted sigh.

'We start at six on Fridays...' I explain regrettably, feeling genuinely sorry for him.

With a thin smile in response, he turns around and reaches for the door handle.

'Wait!' I shout, a little louder than I intended.

Stopping in his tracks, Aidan looks over his shoulder expectantly.

'We have an online support group that could help you until the next meeting, if you're interested?'

We hold eye contact until it becomes uncomfortable, before he finally nods and allows the door to close. Motioning for him to follow me, I lead him into the meeting room, where a few of the others are still talking by the coffee machine. Clearly feeling awkward, Aidan holds back as I grab the forum details from the filing cabinet.

'Here you go.' Holding out the sheet of paper, I point to the website address. 'It's super easy. You just go to this site, create a username and start interacting. Ninety percent of the people here use the forum, so there's always someone online to speak to.'

Opening his mouth to speak, Aidan closes it again as the last of the attendees say their goodbyes and squeeze past us.

'I have the room for another five minutes, if there's anything in particular you would like to talk about?' I offer, studying his face carefully.

Once again, Aidan pauses before shaking his head. 'You don't need to do that. I'll just come along to the next meeting...'

'Are you sure?' I take a step back and point to the empty circle. 'A problem shared is a problem halved.'

He frowns and hesitantly pulls out a chair, letting out a groan that makes my bones ache. Cautiously taking a seat opposite him, I give him a moment to compose himself.

'Anything you say here is completely confidential...'

'I just want to feel normal again.' He whispers, angst ringing through his voice as he stares down at the ground.

Not wanting to push him to the point he closes up, I choose my words carefully. 'And what is normal?'

'I don't know.' He eventually mutters. 'I don't even know who I am anymore.' Running his fingers through his hair, he frowns and closes his eyes. 'Sometimes, I don't even know my own name...'

Nodding along as he speaks, I lick my lips before talking. 'I know it might seem hard to accept, but anxiety and depression don't define who you are. They're things that you have, they're not who you are...'

'Then who am I?' He fires back, bringing his eyes up to meet mine. 'Please, tell me, because the person staring back at me in the mirror isn't me.'

Desperation fills the room as he speaks. He's literally begging me to fix him and tell him that I have the exact remedy he's looking for. My mind flits back to the day that I was in Aidan's shoes and sorrow washes over me.

I open my mouth to speak, but stop myself when the door swings open and Cynthia, the cleaner, pops her head into the room. Happily waving her feather duster in the air, she frowns when she spots us.

'Oh, I'm so sorry for interrupting.' Propping a vacuum cleaner against the wall, she pulls on a pair of gloves. 'I was told this room would be vacant from seven.'

Aidan blinks repeatedly and hastily composes himself. 'I'm sorry for keeping you...'

Pushing himself to his feet, he picks up his backpack and quickly heads for the exit.

'Wait!' I try to run after him, but he slips through the door before I can catch up.

Oblivious to the tension in the air, Cynthia grabs a bottle of polish and hums to herself as she gets to work. Flashing her a strained smile, I sigh heavily and watch Aidan march across the car park, before disappearing out of view. His words ring around my mind as I stand frozen to the spot.

I just want to feel normal again...

Cynthia cleans around me as I silently replay our brief conversation. During my darkest days, I would have given everything I had to feel like my normal self again, but what exactly is *normal?* If we didn't comply to fit in with what society perceives to be normal, how different would our lives look like? How much of what we say, think and feel is orchestrated to fit in with this mould that has been forced upon us?

I was once told, if you're always trying to be normal, you will never know how amazing you can truly be, but what if normality is simply all that you crave?

Chapter 8

Applying the final touches to my makeup, I curse as Mateo jumps onto my lap, causing me to smudge my lipstick. Every time I try to leave the house, it's the same thing. It's almost as though he knows I'm making a bid for freedom and hopes his *please cuddle me* routine will be enough to make me stay. Unfortunately for Mateo, the taxi shall be here at any moment to take us to Ruby's mother's party.

'Your hair has dropped again!' Aldo groans, stepping into the bedroom and immediately grabbing a can of hairspray. 'I told you to leave it alone!'

Watching him expertly backcomb my hair into the perfect chignon, I smile as he pulls a few loose tendrils around my face. Having a hairdresser to the stars as a best friend does have its perks, especially when you have an event to attend. Nodding in satisfaction, he quickly checks his own locks as our cab pulls up outside. With a final look in the mirror, I follow Aldo down the stairs and climb into the waiting taxi.

After giving the address to the driver, I sit back in my seat and pretend to listen as Aldo tells me about his day with the client from hell. A beautiful display of leaves flashes by the windows until we come to London Road. The glitzy row of shops and restaurants twinkle back at me as we shoot by, each one littered with happy tourists enjoying the sunshine.

Speeding down the busy road, it's not long before we leave the bustling street behind and turn onto a country lane. This is what I love the most about living in Alderley Edge. To the left, you have socialites and champagne and to the right, you have sprawling countryside, which is exactly where we are heading. You see, Ruby lives in Mobberley, on her parent's farm and I'm so excited to discover more about her home life. Although we have grown close over the past six months, this will be the first time that Aldo and I have been to her place.

The driver takes a sharp left and pulls onto a secluded path. Feeling the car tremble beneath our feet as we race over uneven ground, I strain my neck for a better view. Spotting an isolated building up ahead, I shield my eyes from the sun. The old farm house stands alone in an extensive open field, brightly decorated in banners and ribbons. Hovering over the seatbelt buckle, a shiver of excitement runs through me as the cab comes to an abrupt stop.

Leaving Aldo to settle the bill, I slide over the seat and step out of the car. Quickly realising I have worn the worst shoes possible for a trip to a farm, I head for the gravel trail and take in my surroundings. Ruby wasn't lying when she said she lived in the middle of nowhere. Apart from a derelict-looking structure opposite, there really is nothing as far as the eye can see.

Mesmerised by the bright rapeseed fields, I almost don't hear Aldo calling my name.

'Earth to Shirley!' Striding ahead, he waves his arms around above his head to gain my attention.

Tearing my eyes away from the blanket of yellow, I hitch up my dress and carefully make my way to the barn conversion. The sound of laughter and upbeat music becomes louder as we rap on the iron knocker. Almost immediately, the door swings open and a gasp escapes my lips.

Standing in front of me is Ruby's double. From the aubergine waves to the big green eyes and porcelain skin, she is an exact replica of the girl I have grown to love. Too busy gawking at the pretty lady, it takes me a moment to realise that this woman is actually twenty years Ruby's senior.

Clearly confused, her gaze moves from Aldo to me and back again as she tries to work out who we are.

'You made it!' A familiar voice shouts over her shoulder, before Ruby pops her head around the doorframe. 'Mum, this is Sadie and Aldo. Guys, this is my mum, Yvette.'

'Happy Birthday!' I exclaim, digging around in my handbag for the card I stuffed in there earlier. 'It's a pleasure to finally meet you!'

Casually taking the pink envelope, Yvette tucks it under her arm and holds out a hand for a polite shake.

'Thank you for coming along.' She smiles thinly and takes my hand in hers. 'Ruby has told me so much about you both.'

'All good things, I hope?' Aldo winks and passes Yvette a bottle of bubbles as we step inside.

'Of course!' She replies, motioning to the pop-up bar at the opposite side of the barn conversion. 'Please, help yourselves to a drink.'

Smoothing down her dress, Yvette excuses herself to greet other guests.

'You and your mother look so alike...' I remark, watching Yvette laugh and giggle in the exact same way Ruby does. 'You could be sisters.'

'Don't let her hear you say that.' Ruby rolls her eyes and beckons us to follow her to the bar. 'I'll never hear the end of it.'

I grin in response as we weave through the clusters of party people. Yvette is nothing like I imagined. From what Ruby has told me, I was expecting a tweed-wearing country lady, who cooked wholesome family meals whilst her husband and sons took care of the farm. In reality, Yvette Robinson is a power-dressing woman with an almost frosty air about her.

As I study Yvette's mannerisms, the music turns up a notch, effectively popping my thought bubble. There was a time where social situations like this would make me want to run for the hills, but now that I have my anxiety under control, I can see it for what it is. No longer do I hyperventilate as that all-encompassing fear grips my chest. The nauseating feeling that used to wash over me when I stepped into a busy room has vanished and fingers crossed, it won't ever come back.

Looking around the party as Ruby nips behind the bar to grab a couple of drinks, I smile to myself at the kitted out barn conversion. Balloons dance happily against the vaulted ceiling, birthday bunting is draped along the walls and every person in the room is wearing a paper party hat. There's no secret surrounding what is happening here today.

Accepting a plastic flute of fizz, I clink it against Aldo's and silently pray we have escaped the dreaded party hats. As though reading my mind, Ruby reaches above the bar and giggles.

'Here you go, guys!' Waving two yellow hats around playfully, she forces one onto my head and hands the other to Aldo. 'You're not part of the family without one.'

Scowling at the silly hat, Aldo shakes out his man-bun and reluctantly tugs the elastic beneath his chin.

'There you go!' Ruby chuckles and claps her hands together. 'You're officially one of the Robinsons!'

Aldo shoots me a glare as I snap a photo of him on my phone and double over with laughter.

'Come on, let me introduce you to the rest of the family...'

Chapter 9

Resting my hands on my hips, I wipe my sweaty brow and take a step back from the makeshift dance floor. Aldo may have the energy levels of a hyper toddler, but two hours of dancing has left me absolutely exhausted.

'I'm just going to get some air!' I yell to Ruby, who is enthusiastically throwing shapes with Aldo. 'I won't be long.'

Nodding in response, Ruby cheers loudly as the music changes track. Plucking my bag from the pile by the bar, I leave the dancers to enjoy the DJ and slip outside. The cool air hits me immediately, providing much-needed relief from the warm room. Taking a few deep breaths, I wobble along the gravel path until I reach a wooden gate. Resting my arms on the fence, I allow my eyes to close and fill my lungs with fresh country air. It must be so refreshing to live somewhere like this. To live in a place where you're completely cut off from the rest of civilisation and everything that comes with it. The loud cars, busy shops and lively restaurants suddenly seem a million miles away.

Peeling open my eyes, my gaze lands on the dilapidated building across the road. The old bricks are in desperate need of a clean and the pile of junk in the yard gives the impression it has been empty for many years. Moving closer, my eyes widen in shock as an elderly man steps out of the front door and hangs a tiny sign in the window. Narrowing my eyes, I try to work out the lettering on the faded plaque. *No vacancies.* I let out a gasp as I read the text. I don't know what I'm more shocked about. The fact it's a B&B or the fact people are actually paying to stay there. The place is neglected beyond belief and it's literally in the middle of nowhere.

Before I can tear my eyes away, another silhouette appears and gives the old gentleman a nod. Too intrigued to return to the party, I wait until the figure steps out of the shadows and feel my stomach drop to the floor. Is that... *Aidan?* Completely transfixed, I watch him pull a packet of cigarettes from his pocket and swiftly light up. Wearing the same jacket he wears to the support group, he inhales deeply as he paces back and forth in front of the building. What is he doing here? There must be hundreds of beautiful hotels in Cheshire. Why on earth would he choose this bed and breakfast?

Suddenly looking up, Aidan's face freezes and he stares directly at me. My heart pounds as I debate running back inside to safety, but before I can move a muscle, he holds up a hand in acknowledgment. Feeling frozen to the spot, I slowly manage to raise my arm and wave back. For a moment, we stare at one another in an eerie silence, until Aidan stubs out his cigarette and makes his way towards me.

It seems to take an eternity for him to walk the short distance across the road and when he finally stops on the other side of the gate, you could hear a pin drop.

'Hi.' He mumbles, squinting to avoid being blinded by the bright sun.

Quickly remembering I have a party hat on, I hurriedly snatch it off my head in embarrassment. 'It's a birthday party.' I explain, motioning towards the barn conversion.

'Ah...' Aidan looks behind me, his brow pulled into a tight frown as he stifles a yawn. 'That explains the music that disturbed me.'

I open my mouth to apologise when I realise it's only five in the afternoon.

'You were sleeping?' I ask, before I can stop myself.

Slowly shaking his head in response, Aidan looks away. 'Not unless you class staring at the ceiling in desperation as *sleeping*.'

I offer him a sympathetic smile and peek at the crumbling bed and breakfast.

Following my gaze, Aidan turns to look at the tired structure. 'It's not as bad as it looks.'

I try to appear convinced, but my scepticism shines through.

'Honestly...' He protests, shoving his hands into his pockets. 'I can show you, if you like?'

I glance over my shoulder at the barn conversion and bite my lip. I should politely decline and head back to the party, but something inside me wants to find out more about him. If I know more about Aidan, maybe it will enable me to help him more at the support group.

'Okay.' I reply, trying to sound casual as I fasten my hat to the fence. 'They won't miss me for five minutes.'

Fumbling with a hidden latch on the left side of the panel, Aidan holds open the gate and allows it to close behind me. A light wind whooshes past us as I follow him across the grass and towards the B&B. The closer

I get, I notice he's right. It's not as bad as it first looked. A few sporadic cars are parked in the yard and a couple of other guests are sat in the overgrown garden behind the building. Yes, it's tired, but I can now see it's a fully functioning establishment.

Watching Aidan reach for the door handle, I can't help noticing that his right hand is badly bruised and covered in scratches. Frowning in confusion, I choose not to draw attention to it and step inside. The first thing that hits me is the musty smell that hangs thickly in the air. You know the kind, the smell you only find in charity shops that sticks in the back of your throat like smog.

'It's this way.' Aidan points to a set of stairs and fishes a key out of his jacket.

The carpet feels sparse beneath my feet as I follow him up the creaky steps. Each one groans louder than the last until we come to a stop at an old wooden door. Overlooking the peeling wallpaper, I hold my breath and cautiously step inside. It's only when the door slams shut behind me that my warning senses kick in. What am I doing? I've followed a mysterious man, who has obviously punched a wall, into a falling down B&B without telling a soul.

'Well, what do you think?' He asks, standing in front of the only window and effectively blocking out all the light.

Trying not to panic, I lick my dry lips and look around the room. The four-poster bed is heavily scratched, with a wonky headboard and faded floral duvet. Retro lamps sit on the dusty windowsills and it's fair to say that the dated bathroom has seen better days.

'It's... *nice*.' I manage, trying my hardest to sound genuine.

A tiny smile washes over Aidan's face before his frown returns. 'I wouldn't go that far, but I needed a room and they had a vacancy.'

Nodding in response, I fumble with the hem of my sleeve nervously. 'What brings you to Mobberley?' I ask, completely flummoxed as to why anyone would stumble across this place.

'I have no idea.' He mutters, his voice barely audible. 'I just walked.'

'Walked from where?' Desperate for him to elaborate, I take a step towards him.

Taking a seat on the edge of the bed, Aidan holds his head in his hands. 'I just had to get away. I needed to be somewhere people didn't know my name.'

Gingerly edging closer, I perch on the duvet next to him, not wanting to interrupt his flow.

'I couldn't take it anymore. I couldn't take the questions, the sympathetic looks and the constant memories...' His voice trails off and he takes a deep breath. 'I thought I could run away from the gut-wrenching hollowness inside, but it's followed me. It's still here and it's getting darker with every day that passes.'

I've lost count of the number of people I've met at Anxiety Anonymous who have tried to run away from their problems. From last-minute trips to the Caribbean, to hastily-ended relationships and snap decisions they believe will fix them. Burying your feelings seems the most appealing idea when you're of poor mental health, but sooner or later, that box is going to have to be opened if you stand any chance of moving on and putting it behind you.

'It will pass.' I say gently, studying every line on his face. 'That seems hard to believe right now, but it will.'

'I used to believe that, but as time ticks by, I'm beginning to lose hope I will ever be *me* again...'

'Have you had any professional help for the way you're feeling?' I ask, noticing a white strip of skin on his wedding finger where a ring used to sit.

Aidan shakes his head slowly and rubs his eyes in frustration. 'No. I thought I could handle this myself.'

'There's no shame in admitting you're struggling. Every single person at the support group has been where you are now. They have all had to make the decision to ask for help and that is the first step on the road back to recovery. Until you admit that to yourself, you'll forever be taking one step forward and two steps back.'

There's an emotional silence, before Aidan clears his throat and speaks up.

'So, if I come back to the support group, you can help me?' He twists his body to face mine, hope carved into his tired face. 'You can take this all away and put me back to the way I was before?'

'I wish it was that simple, I really do.' I sigh heavily and shake my head. 'I can't promise to free you of your troubles until you have addressed the root cause yourself. The door to Anxiety Anonymous will always be open, you just have to choose to walk through it.'

Aidan stares at me closely, before eventually nodding. Hoping I have given him the push that he needs, I steal a glimpse at my watch and push myself up.

'I should be getting back to the party...'

'Yes, of course.' Aidan quickly composes himself and pulls open the door. 'Thank you for taking the time to talk to me.'

'You're most welcome.' I give him a friendly smile and make for the stairs, stopping as I reach for the wobbly rail. 'So, will we be seeing you at the next meeting?'

Aidan scratches his stubble and nods, signalling an end to our bizarre conversation. Carefully treading down the noisy steps, I push my way outside and head across the field. Music from the party fills the air as I release the fence and untie my hat from the post. Slipping it onto my head, I hitch up my dress and tread across the gravel, giving the B&B a final glance before walking back into the barn conversion.

Ruby and Aldo are still rocking the dance floor, although now they have a crowd of cheering people egging them on. Giving them a little wave, I lean against the bar and join in with the jovialities. Thankfully, they haven't even realised I've been missing, which is something I am incredibly grateful for. Aldo already treats me with kid gloves. I can just imagine the ear-bashing I would get if I told him where I've really been. Following a clearly troubled man into a neglected building probably isn't the smartest thing I've ever done, but my inner anxiety girl is longing to help him.

Since the day I signed my contract with Anxiety Anonymous, I promised myself I would give everything I had to the role and if that means going above and beyond the call of duty, so be it. I'll never forget feeling as horrifically low as Aidan feels right now and if I can help to free him from the mental torture that is slowly destroying him, *nothing* will stop me from doing it...

Chapter 10

Fishing through the plastic box, I dig out a peg and clip the final towel to the washing line. Watching the rows of clothes billowing in the warm breeze, I grab the empty laundry basket and take a seat on the bench. All morning I have washed, dried and pressed load after load of laundry. Transforming the wrinkly garments into freshly-ironed outfits gives me immense satisfaction. Removing the crumples makes me feel like I have my life in order. After all, with no creases in your clothes, you will only have wrinkles where your smiles have been.

Since my spontaneous meeting with Aidan yesterday, I haven't been able to shake him from my mind. In one way or another, every person I come into contact with at Anxiety Anonymous makes a lasting impression on me, but Aidan has bothered me more than anyone has before. The heartache in his eyes is deeper and darker than I ever thought possible. His pained expression tormented me every time I closed my eyes last night and it was still with me when I rolled out of bed this morning.

Trying to forget about everything work-related, I stand up to head inside when Mateo strolls out of the kitchen. Pausing to rub his head on the bench, he purrs gently and pads his way over to me. Taking a moment to check the perimeters of his precious garden, he lets out a *meow* and rolls onto his back.

After giving him a quick belly rub, I leave him to bask in the sunshine and pick up the empty basket.

The kitchen is warm from the strong sun as I pull a notepad from the cupboard and start to make a list. Since the day I moved into Blossom View, I have been making a mental note of the many things that need painting, plastering and perfecting. Now that I've settled in, it's finally time to address them. Tapping the pen against the paper, I move from room to room and make messy squiggles on the page. When I finally stop, I am faced with a list longer than my arm and I must admit to feeling a little overwhelmed.

Grabbing my laptop, I scour the internet for some of the problems I have found and feel my heart drop. Obviously, I planned on giving the cottage a facelift, but according to this, the cracks in the walls are going to take a lot more than a quick lick of paint to fix. Running my eyes over the text, I try and fail to work out where to start. Maybe I should call in a builder. Someone who can put a plan together to whip this place into shape. Sometimes, the best course of action is to take a step back and leave it to the professionals.

Chewing the end of my pen, I close the computer and scour the television cabinet for the Yellow Pages. Finally locating it beneath a stash of Christmas cards, I flip through the pages and stop when I hear Mateo meowing loudly from the garden. Abandoning the directory, I quickly find him sprawled out in the same strip of sunshine on the grass. Taking a seat next to him, I lie back and bask in the vitamin D.

Glancing over at the seeds Aldo and I planted a few days ago, I'm reminded of his offer to set me up with one of his clients. It's been so long since I enjoyed the company of another man. Well, one who doesn't have a boyfriend of his own, anyway. A part of me is petrified of opening my heart to another person, but deep down, I would give anything to share my life with someone. Someone who will laugh with me in the good times and help me through the bad is what has been missing from my life. I'm just terrified of allowing it to happen.

I look down at my finger tattoo and try to convince myself that not every relationship ends in disaster. Am I afraid of falling in love again, or am I afraid of the heartache that could cause me to tumble back into the grips of anxiety? There are people out there who fall in love with one another day after day, year after year. Real love *does* exist. The question is, am I willing to lower my guard enough to let it happen for me?

Rolling onto my stomach, I pluck a blade of glass and twirl it around my fingers. Maybe I should listen to my own advice and face my fears. What's the worst that could happen if I take Aldo up on his offer and meet his mystery man for a drink? One of the things I learned in training, is to take each daunting experience and use it as an opportunity to test your power over anxiety. Despite saying this on a daily basis, I still find it difficult to put into practice. Regardless of what you're afraid of, facing your fears is always easier said than done.

Before I can stop it, my mind drifts to Aidan and I wonder if he will be strong enough to face *his* own fears. Acknowledging that you aren't coping can seem such a monumental thing to admit. Telling another person your mind is effectively broken is a terrifying thing to do, but it's essential if you want to recover. I just hope that Aidan gets the courage to save himself, before he falls any deeper...

* * *

Brushing my fingers across the red cushion, I clear my throat and run my eyes around the room. The meeting started ten minutes ago and I've spent at least eight of those staring at Aidan. Unlike the last meeting, he seems on high alert. Perched on the edge of his seat, he is soaking up my every word like a sponge.

'As I explained earlier, we're going to do things a little differently today.' Holding up the tiny pillow, I smile at the confused faces staring back at me. 'This is our release cushion, which we are going to pass around the room. Once you are in possession of the cushion, you can choose to speak or you can simply pass it to the next person.' I pause and turn over the cushion in my hands. 'There are no rules regarding what you speak about. If you're having a terrible day, feel free to express your emotion. Alternatively, if you have discovered a new way to control your anxiety, please share this, so others can have the same success as you. Anything goes. Whether it be good, bad, happy or sad.'

A few people nod along as I wait for any questions before handing the cushion to the man at the far right of the circle. The biggest obstacle I face when counselling these support groups is getting people to talk. After various techniques and failed methods at coaxing them to speak, I am hoping my release cushion will have better results.

The first man holds the cushion sceptically for a moment, before swiftly handing it to the next person. My heart drops as the pillow is quickly passed around the circle like a hot potato. I watch in dismay as the cushion makes it halfway around the group, before coming to a stop in the lap of a young man I don't recognise. Exhaling loudly, he leans back in his seat and taps his foot anxiously.

'I'm struggling...' He starts, refusing to make eye contact with anything other than the pillow. 'We recently moved into the area and I'm finding it really difficult to adjust.'

I smile at him and nod, waiting for him to elaborate. 'I never used to be like this. I had a huge group of friends back in Newcastle, but since the move, I've just wanted to stay at home. My dad tells me I will make new friends, but I'm not interested in meeting new people. I just want my old life back.'

His floppy hair falls into his face as his cheeks flush pink.

'I lie awake all night, praying to be in my old house when I open my eyes, but of course, I never am. My parents don't realise how much I'm struggling. The first and last time I told them how I felt, they smothered me for a week. Their constant questions and sympathetic looks made me feel even worse. Every day seems to get tougher, I just don't want to be here. It's affecting my grades and it's making me more miserable than I ever knew possible.'

Finally looking up, he peeks around the room and immediately sits up straight. 'Sorry, did I share too much?'

'You can *never* share too much.' I say softly, offering him a reassuring smile.

'I just feel so stupid.' He continues, running his fingers over the cushion. 'All we did was move. I mean, it's not the end of the world. People move all the time, don't they? Why can't I just deal with it?'

'You don't need to justify why you are having a hard time. We're all different, we all react to things in different ways. Just because other people adjust faster than you, doesn't mean that they're right and you're wrong.'

He nods in agreement and chews at his thumbnail nervously.

'It's perfectly okay to admit that you're finding it difficult to adjust to your new surroundings. Try not to be so hard on yourself. As time passes, you *will* settle in your new home.'

The young boy manages a small smile and breathes a sigh of relief, clearly comforted by sharing his problem with someone who understands.

'Don't be afraid to confide in your parents, friends and other family members. You might feel as though allowing them in will make your situation worse, but those who care about you will want to do everything they can to help you.'

Smiling back at me, he hands the release cushion to Aidan and looks at him expectantly.

Go on, I beg silently. *I can't help you if you don't talk to me.* Mentally willing him to let go of his reservations, I bite my lip as Aidan opens and closes his mouth repeatedly. Scratching his beard, he shakes his head in annoyance and finally passes the pillow to the person on his right. My heart sinks in my chest as disappointment fills his eyes. I've seen that look so many times before. The look that says, *I hate myself for not speaking, but I'm afraid of what might happen if I let the words slip out.*

Fixing my face into a smile, I try to focus as a familiar lady shares her success story with calming apps. Aidan's refusal to let people in is frustrating, but you can't push someone up a ladder, unless they are ready to climb...

Chapter 11

Saying goodbye to Alec, I intentionally take longer than necessary to button up my cardigan. Just like the last time, Aidan is deliberately hanging back, clearly waiting for the rest of the group to leave. Taking the hint that he's waiting to talk to me, I hover by the information stand until the room empties. Hearing the final footsteps fade into silence, I step towards him and tug my handbag onto my shoulder.

'How did you find the meeting?' I ask, leaning against the stand of pamphlets.

'Great.' He replies awkwardly, running a hand through his hair. 'Really great.'

I smile back at him, sensing that he's gearing up to say something. The words are on the tip of his tongue, itching to make a bid for freedom.

'I couldn't do it...' He whispers in frustration, cracking his knuckles angrily. 'I wanted to. I really did. I just couldn't bring myself to say it.'

'To say what?' I press gently, realising I'm holding my breath.

'All of it.' Throwing his arms in the air, he paces back and forth. 'I don't even know where to start. How do I know if I am sharing too much or not enough? I don't know what parts I should say and what parts I should keep to myself...'

'There's no pressure.' I interrupt, holding up a hand to stop him. 'You don't have to say anything at all. Not now, not ever, if you don't want to.'

My heart pangs with sadness as his eyes glass over.

'There's no rule book when it comes to matters of the mind. There's no right or wrong way to deal with it. Some people come here and get everything off their chest in one session, others don't breathe a word for months on end. Just trust your instinct. When you're ready to talk, we will be here. Like I said, our door is always open.'

Aidan turns to look out of the window and nods half-heartedly. 'The sun is shining.' He observes, leaning over and twisting the blinds open.

'It is.' Slightly bemused by his sudden change of subject, I decide to drop the counselling and go with it. 'It looks like it's going to be a beautiful day.'

'Make the most of it.' Leaning against the wall, Aidan watches the world rush past the window. 'Storms are forecast for tomorrow.'

I let out a little groan and rub my temples. 'Well, that's my plans ruined.'

Aidan shoots me a questioning look and I clear my throat.

'I have a whole bunch of building work that needs carrying out.' I explain, straightening a wonky leaflet on the information stand. 'I intended to call a builder and have them take a look around, but I should probably leave it until Wednesday.'

'Have you already hired someone?' Aidan asks, sounded genuinely intrigued.

'Not yet. To be honest, I don't even know where to start. I recently bought a house and it needs so much more work doing than I originally anticipated.'

'I could take a look for you.' Aidan's cheeks flush violently the second the words escape his lips.

'Really?' I reply, touched by his kind offer. 'Are you a builder?'

'I am. Or rather, I *was...*' Suddenly looking rather uncomfortable, he starts to backtrack. 'Actually, forget I said anything. It was inappropriate of me to offer.'

'No!' I exclaim, shaking my head. 'You would be doing me a huge favour.'

Aidan hesitates, before mumbling something that resembles *okay*. Taking a pamphlet, I quickly scribble down my address and hand it to him. Gently accepting the leaflet, Aidan folds it carefully and places it in his top pocket.

'Thank you so much for this. I really appreciate it.' Motioning to the clock on the wall, I start walking towards the door. 'I'm sorry I can't stay and chat. I'm meeting a friend for dinner.'

Giving me a swift nod, Aidan falls into step next to me as we make our way outside and across the car park.

'I'm this way.' Pointing towards Grove Street, I smile at Aidan as he tilts his head in the opposite direction.

'I guess I shall see you tomorrow then.' Already knowing that he's probably heading straight back to the bed and breakfast, I give him a final wave and watch him walk away.

As I head towards the restaurant, where I have arranged to meet Ruby, a familiar voice catches my attention. Looking up, my lips stretch into a smile as I see her walking towards me. Wearing her favourite biker boots and a cute tea dress, she waves manically as she comes to a stop in front of me.

'Hey!' Ruby grins widely and gestures behind me. 'Who's the guy?'

Not wanting to look back, I shrug my shoulders and link my arm through hers. 'Just someone from the support group.'

Before she can quiz me further, I lead her into the restaurant and drop my bag onto our favourite table.

'Thanks again for inviting us to the party.' I gush, sliding into my seat. 'Aldo and I had so much fun.'

'My family didn't scare you off?' Pulling a funny face, Ruby positions a cushion behind her back and makes a grab for the menu.

'Not at all!' I retort, quickly ordering a couple of drinks with the waitress. 'Your mum is so cool.'

'*Cool* being the operative word.' Ruby laughs and checks her hair for split ends. 'She can come across a little frosty sometimes, but she's not all that bad.'

'Frosty?' I repeat, pretending I didn't notice Yvette's reserved manner at the party. 'What do you mean?'

'It's just the way that she is.' Ruby explains, studying the menu closely. 'I've grown used to it, but her detached personality doesn't help when my anxiety strikes. I don't think she realises how lonely her lack of emotion makes me feel. We can be in the same room as one another, yet I will feel more alone than ever.'

A lump forms in my throat and I try to disguise it behind a forced smile. Completely oblivious to the fact she's just told me one of the saddest things I've ever heard, Ruby taps her fingers on the table as she reels off the menu choices. My relationship with my own mother is far from perfect, but the idea of Ruby feeling like her mum has no compassion for her is heart-breaking. No wonder she's suffered with her mental health for so long.

'Is your dad as *cool* as your mum?' I ask, realising I didn't say more than two words to him at the party.

'My dad just does whatever my mum tells him to.' She giggles and tosses her hair over her shoulder. 'It's my mum who wears the trousers.'

I join in with her laughter as two steaming mugs are placed on the table. I often wonder about my own dad. I've never known my father. Apart from a fleeting conversation, where he had absolutely no idea who I was, we've never been introduced. My biological makeup has played on my mind a lot this past year, but I've finally convinced myself that you can't miss something you never had.

'So, did you get a quote for the work on Blossom View?' Ruby asks, tapping out a message on her phone.

Sipping my drink slowly, I consider telling her about Aidan, but something inside me decides against it. 'Someone's coming tomorrow to have a look around. I'll have a better idea after that.'

Twirling a ring around her finger, Ruby rests her chin in her palm. 'How are you finding the cottage?'

'It's great. It feels as though I've always been there.' I look down into my coffee and watch steam rise from the hot mug. 'It's like my old life doesn't exist anymore. Life really started for me when I got the keys to Blossom View.'

Sighing happily, my smile falters when I realise Ruby is frowning back at me.

'You haven't had a visit from *Ann* since you moved, have you?' She lowers her voice to a whisper, obviously wanting to keep our conversation hushed from the rest of the restaurant.

Naming my anxiety was the best tip I was ever given, even if it does make it look as though I'm talking to myself sometimes.

'No.' I reply confidently. 'And if she does, you shall be the first to know.'

Ruby and Aldo can't seem to accept that since my brief spell with anxiety I haven't had a relapse, but the truth is, I haven't. I still find it hard to believe myself. There are some mornings where I wake up, fully expecting to feel that emptiness inside me, but it never comes. I can honestly say that as of right now, I'm free from fear, free from anxiety and free from Ann...

Chapter 12

Ushering Mateo to the floor, I wander over to the window and watch the rain lash against the cloudy glass. The sky is a dark shade of grey, which is only broken up by the odd bolt of lightning. When I rolled out of bed this morning, I quickly realised I didn't arrange a time with Aidan to come over today. I also realised I had no means of contacting him to find out and after two hours of watching the horrendous weather outside, I'm not holding my breath.

Just as I'm considering giving up, there's a knock at the door. Frowning in confusion, I press my nose against the window to get a glimpse of my visitor through the driving rain. Not being able to see anything more than a wet blur, I jog along the lobby and throw open the door.

'Aidan!' I exclaim, my jaw dropping to the floor as I take in his drenched appearance. 'Oh, my goodness! Come inside.'

Smiling gratefully, he attempts to shake the excess water out of his hair before stepping into the hallway. His clothes are saturated from the rain, causing wet droplets to form a perfect circle around him.

'You're soaked!' Dashing into the kitchen, I grab a couple of towels from the laundry basket.

'I know. It's a long walk from the bus stop.' Accepting a towel, he peels off his jacket and wipes himself down.

'You walked in the rain?' I ask in bewilderment, hanging his coat over the radiator to dry off. 'Why didn't you get a taxi?'

'I like walking.' Folding the towel neatly, he hands it back to me and looks around the lobby.

Before I can question his bizarre decision to walk two miles in torrential conditions, he snaps into work mode.

'So, what exactly is it you want me to look at?'

Grabbing the list I wrote from the cabinet, my cheeks turn pink as he squints at the messy scribbles. 'Please excuse my terrible handwriting.'

He forces a thin smile and taps the paper with a stubby pencil. 'Is it okay to have a look around?'

'Of course.' I reply, gesturing for him to make himself at home. 'Can I get you a drink? Tea? Coffee?'

'I'm fine, thank you.' Taking the list with him, he gives me a polite nod and disappears into the living room.

With a final glance at his wet jacket, I make my way into the kitchen and flick on the kettle. When Aidan offered to call over today, I pictured him arriving in a white van with a pair of shoddy overalls. Between you and me, I'm a little concerned about how much work he can carry out with a solitary pencil that has seen better days.

Taking my mug, I walk into the living room and watch Aidan run his fingers along the cracks in the wall, taking care not to tread on a purring Mateo.

'He's not bothering you, is he?' I ask, attempting to coax my over-friendly cat away.

Aidan shakes his head and bends down to stroke him. Happily lapping up the attention, Mateo *meows* like the cat who got the cream as he rubs his head around Aidan's ankles.

'Are you an animal lover?' Perching on the end on the couch, I fluff up the cushions behind me. 'Since having Mateo, I feel like a house is not a home without a cat.'

'I was never home long enough to have a pet.' Aidan gives him a final stroke, before pulling back the curtains to assess the window frames. 'Work took up the majority of my time.'

'Where is home?' I reply, already knowing that his accent sounds far from local.

He visibly flinches and makes a scribble on the paper I gave him. 'Surrey.' He says eventually, an edge to his voice that I haven't heard before.

I want to ask what brings him to a neglected B&B in rural Mobberley, but the counsellor in me warns against it. I've slowly realised this is Aidan's way of communicating. Revealing tiny pieces of information before snapping shut is a pattern of his.

'Did you have a survey done before you bought this place?' He mumbles, kneeling down and prodding at the skirting board with the end of his pencil.

'Of course...' I walk over to the drawers and rifle through the stacks of paperwork. 'Here it is.'

Taking the documentation, Aidan flips through the pages and frowns. 'This a valuation report. You did get a full structural survey, right?'

'No.' I chew the inside of my cheek anxiously and frown. 'The guy who carried out the report didn't advise further investigations. He had a quick look around and said this was all I'd need considering I wasn't getting a mortgage.'

'Technically, he was right, but you shouldn't ever purchase a property without having it fully checked out.'

I mumble in agreement, really not liking the direction in which this conversation is going.

Beckoning me to follow him, Aidan kneels onto the rug and motions to the skirting board. 'It looks like you've got rising damp.'

'Rising damp?' I reach out and touch the wood, before letting out a gasp as it crumbles from my touch. 'What does that even mean?'

'It means you're going to need a damp-proof course, but I should warn you, they can be expensive.' Offering his hand to help me to my feet, he points to the floorboards. 'These will polish up beautifully.'

I nod in agreement, trying not to show how disappointed I am for making such a rookie mistake.

'How long have you been here?' He asks, taking my mind off the dreaded damp.

'Not long, I used to live in the apartments down the lane.' Picking up Mateo, I scratch him behind the ears as he gets comfortable in my arms. 'Are you familiar with the area?'

'Not at all. I've only been up here for a couple of weeks...' Writing numbers on the sheet of paper, he ventures into the kitchen and knocks on the partition wall. 'Personally, I would take this down. It would free up all of this space.'

'What brings you to Cheshire?' I interject, the words tumbling out of my mouth before I can stop them. 'At the B&B, you said you *walked* to Mobberley.'

'I needed a change of scenery, so I just packed a bag and walked to the train station.' Aidan pauses, his pencil pressed to the page. 'When it first happened, I tried so hard to carry on, but as the days turned into months, I realised I couldn't stay there a moment longer. I jumped on the very first train that came into the station. Hours passed as I stared out of the window, changing trains at random. I only disembarked when they announced their final stop.'

I lean against the counter, completely mesmerised by what he is saying.

'When I walked out of the station, I had two choices, left or right. I've always tried to do the right thing in life and it hasn't done me any favours, so I chose left. I walked for miles, following the public footpaths through fields and country lanes until the sun started to set. The B&B was the first place I came to where I could rest my head for the night.'

Aidan's eyes glass over as he gives me a rare insight into his life.

'I left everything behind. If it didn't fit into my suitcase, I was going without it. I told myself, as long as I had the stars above me and some money in my pocket I would be fine, but a week of being alone with my thoughts drove me insane. I just had to get out of there.'

There's a wobble in his voice, but he disguises it with a forced cough.

'Venturing back into civilisation was harder than I anticipated. The people, the chaos and the mayhem of everyday life made me feel claustrophobic. I just stood in the middle of the street as panic took over my body. That's when I saw the sign for Anxiety Anonymous. It was like someone, *somewhere*, was throwing me a lifeline. If I wouldn't have walked through that door, I don't know what I would have done...'

A look of relief creeps onto his face at finally getting a little of his story off his chest.

'What happened?' I whisper, inching towards him. 'What caused you to walk away from your life like that?'

Aidan stares directly at me, neither of us daring to breathe as he prepares himself to reveal what brought him here. Hearing the front door squeak open, I snap back to attention as Aldo's voice drifts into the kitchen.

'Shirley?'

'In here!' I yell, my voice coming out a little higher than I intended.

Looking at Aidan as Aldo's footsteps echo along the lobby, I smile apologetically.

'Hey!' Taking off his jacket, Aldo throws his keys onto the dining table and heads straight for the fridge. 'You finally hired a builder...'

'I did.' I glance at Aidan, who returns to his list and inspects the back door carefully, obviously not wanting to make small talk. 'Let's go into the living room and give him some space to work.'

Striding out of the kitchen, I wait until Aldo curls up on the couch before shutting the door quietly.

'Where did you find the builder?' He asks, kicking off his shoes and reaching for the remote control. 'I didn't notice a van outside.'

'He didn't come in a van.' I say breezily, really hoping he drops the subject of Aidan. 'He walked...'

'He walked?' Frowning in confusion, Aldo flicks through the TV channels. 'How did he carry his tools?'

Tickling Mateo under the chin, I shrug my shoulders and pretend to be engrossed in the television. 'He didn't bring any tools.'

Hitting *pause* on the remote, Aldo turns to face me, his blue eyes narrowed. 'A builder with no van and no tools? What's going on?'

'Aidan's from the support group...' I explain, trying to keep my voice to a whisper. 'I mentioned I was looking for a builder and he offered to have a look around...'

'You're kidding, right?' Aldo cuts me off mid-sentence with an expression I can't quite read.

'It's not a big deal...' I protest, hitting *play* on the remote control.

'It's a *huge* deal! Aldo hisses, suddenly becoming rather angry. 'What do you even know about this guy?'

'His name is Aidan...'

Shaking his head incredulously, Aldo slides over the couch until he is sat just inches away from me. 'You have invited a complete stranger into your home! Do you have any idea how dangerous this could potentially be? I thought the whole point of Anxiety Anonymous was to be *anonymous*...'

Becoming increasingly worried that Aidan is going to overhear us, I motion for him to lower his voice. 'You're blowing this out of proportion. He's just doing me a favour, that's all. The fact he attends the support group is completely irrelevant.'

Aldo opens his mouth to speak, just as Aidan pops his head into the room.

'So, I had a look around and here is what you should expect to pay for the work you itemised.' Handing over the piece of paper, which is now covered in his handwriting, he gives Aldo a polite nod. 'I've highlighted the things I would prioritise, such as the damp we spoke about before.'

'Thank you so much, Aidan. I really appreciate it.'

Taking the list from me, Aldo runs his eyes across the text dubiously. 'How long do you think it will take for you to carry out the work?' He asks, looking Aidan up and down suspiciously.

'Oh, I won't be able to do the work myself.' Aidan says regrettably. 'I'm not working at the moment. I just offered to give Sadie an idea of what needs doing.'

Aldo gives him a wary look and I discreetly kick him under the coffee table, praying that he doesn't give Aidan a hard time.

'I should be going...' Aidan says, breaking the tension by reaching for his backpack.

'Are you sure you won't stay for a drink?' I ask, really not wanting him to leave when we came so close to revealing the truth earlier.

He politely declines and I follow him out into the hallway. 'I'm sorry about Aldo. I didn't realise he would be calling over today.'

'It's fine. I did what I came to do.'

We hold eye contact and I smile back at him, his dark eyes appearing a shade lighter than when he arrived. 'Well, if you ever need a friend, you know where I am.'

With a quick nod, Aidan pulls up his hood and strides down the garden path. Leaning on the doorframe, my heart pangs with sadness as I watch him walk away. He needs help, he needs a hug and more than anything else, he needs a friend. When I was at my lowest point, I had Aldo right by side. He lifted me up when I was down, he ensured I got the help that I needed and he refused to give up on me.

Unfortunately, we're not all lucky enough to have an Aldo. To have that one special person who will stand by us when no one else will is a rare thing. Some people, like Aidan, have to just hope that someone, somewhere, has their back and keep on believing that everything will turn out okay...

Chapter 13

Shoving my feet into my trainers, I fumble with the laces before allowing myself a quick stretch. Today is my day off and with the sun shining brightly, I intend to dedicate the entire twenty-four hours to some much-needed *me* time. Recognising I'm about to leave, Mateo lets out a disappointed *meow*, before retreating into the living room. Leaving him to sulk, I push my way outside and immediately slip on my sunglasses.

Throughout the course of last night, the heavy rain and howling wind slowly subsided and if the warm rays beaming down on me are anything to go by, it looks like we're in for a beautiful day. The blanket of blue above is perfectly clear. There's not a cloud in sight as far as the eye can see. Filling my lungs with fresh air, I pop in my earphones and give a friendly wave to my neighbour across the lane.

Music floods into my ears as I stride past the row of quaint cottages and take a sharp right to cut across the daisy-littered field. The grass is wet beneath my feet as I duck beneath the overgrown trees to join the secluded bridle path. Although I've lived in Alderley Edge for many years, it was only recently that I discovered this particular walkway. Unlike the popular tourist spots, this trail is often secluded. You can walk for hours on end and still not see another person.

With the house move and extensive training courses for Anxiety Anonymous, I haven't had much free time to dedicate to my beloved countryside. Losing myself in the trees and woodland is one of my favourite things to do. There's something quite magical about being completely alone. To be completely at one with nature and detached from the rest of the world is an incredible feeling.

Approaching a tired gate, I pull myself onto the pew and throw my leg over. Landing in a heap on the other side, I dust myself down and carry on. The path ahead becomes wider as I pound against the gravel, pausing only to take a gulp of water from the bottle in my backpack. Wiping my brow, I smile to myself as I spot a couple of ponies in the field to my left. Unable to resist, I push my sunglasses into my hair and stick my hand over the fence. Immediately looking up, a small pony trots towards me.

'Hello.' I whisper, leaning down to stroke his neck.

Rubbing his head against the palm of my hand, the friendly pony gives me a final swish of the tail before returning his attention to the grass.

Continuing on my journey, I breathe in deeply and feel every muscle in my body relax. This is my happy place. Being in the open air gives me a great sense of freedom. It enables me to clear my mind and to free myself from the daily grind that clouds my judgement. It also makes me realise why Aidan feels so comfortable at the B&B.

After Aidan left last night, Aldo and I spent the night on the couch watching movies, just like old times. Sometimes, I miss Aldo so much it actually hurts. Since I sold the apartment, we have both moved on with our lives and inevitably, our friendship has been put on the back-burner ever so slightly. We'll always be incredibly close, that will never change, but I understand why we've had to loosen the strings a little. I've relied on Aldo so much in the past and I guess I always will, but he has more in his life to focus on right now. I know his door will always be open, but now the time has come for me to stand on my own two feet.

A squawking sound behind me catches my attention and I look over my shoulder to see a flock of birds soaring through the sky. Too busy watching them dance on the horizon, it takes me a moment to realise that I've walked further than I ever have before. Not being deterred, I continue ahead and enjoy the sensation of warm sun on my skin.

After a while, the track fizzles out into an arid patch of grass, which finally disappears into the dense cluster of trees. Deciding to see where it goes, I wipe my sweaty brow and duck between the branches. Pushing my way through the untidy bushes, I curse as a nettle scratches my bare ankle. Not being able to see more than a few feet in front of me, I continue to struggle through the forest until I see light in the clearing ahead.

Finally stumbling into sparse grassland, I rest my hands on my knees and try to steady my breathing. Blinking repeatedly, I scour the deserted area for the next public footpath sign. Unable to find one, I turn back and try to retrace my steps. Quickly realising I have taken a wrong turn, I attempt the opposite direction, only to find myself in another isolated area.

Panic rises in my throat as it dawns on me that I don't know where I am. Trying not to freak out, I spin around and take in my surroundings. I can't possibly be lost. I was on the bridle path just a few moments ago! Peering through the leafy branches, my heart starts to pound as I try to think about this clearly. A ten-minute walk in one of four directions will lead me back to the public trail. Taking a stab at right, I shield my face from the spiky twigs and power on through.

Stopping when I spot a patch of flowers I don't recognise, I let out a panicked groan as my ears start to ring. My blood runs cold the second I hear that all-too-familiar sound. The sound that indicates the start of a panic attack makes my stomach churn uncontrollably. Leaning against the trunk of a tree, I feel paralysed with shock. This cannot be happening. I have done with anxiety and panic attacks. I *conquered* anxiety and panic attacks.

Reminding myself that I teach people how to deal with this every day of the week, I squeeze my eyes shut and slowly count to ten. Nausea races through me as my knees start to tremble and my legs become increasingly weak.

'Piss off, Ann.' I hiss, wiping my sweaty hands on my leggings. 'Just leave me alone...'

'I'm sorry?'

Inhaling sharply, I spin around to see an elderly man in a cap peering through the branches in confusion.

'Are you okay?' He asks, pushing his glasses up the bridge of his nose.

The shock of realising I'm not alone brings my panic attack to an abrupt end and I breathe a sigh of relief.

'I'm... I'm lost.' I manage, an embarrassed laugh escaping my lips. 'I followed the path through the trees and now I can't find my way back.'

'Don't worry.' Chuckling heartily, he adjusts his flat cap and pushes a branch back with his walking stick. 'It's easily done out here. I don't normally come this far, but Aloysius decided to go on a little adventure. Oh, look! There he is now...'

A scuffling sound rustles behind me, before a huge Siberian Husky jumps out from between the trees.

'There you are!' The elderly man laughs as Aloysius tucks his tail between his legs guiltily. 'He won't hurt you. He's as timid as a mouse. Aren't you, Aloysius?'

Holding out my hand, I wait for him to inspect it before going in for a stroke. Lapping up the attention, Aloysius wags his tail back and forth manically.

'Do you think you could show me the way back to civilisation, Aloysius?' I ask, crouching down to his level and scratching his chin.

'Don't ask him! He gets lost in the bloody garden.' His owner jokes. 'Come on, love. I'll show you the way.'

Smiling thankfully, I grab my backpack and follow him through the woodland. As my saviour tells me about his life with Aloysius, I nod along and try to ignore the fluttering in my stomach. Although I managed to nip it in the bud before it got out of control, recognising the early signs of a panic attack has unnerved me. Since my breakdown, I haven't had so much as an unpleasant twinge. So, why? Why now? Was that a sign of things to come, or merely an example of how panic and anxiety are normal emotions in potentially dangerous situations?

I'd convinced myself that my brush with anxiety was short-lived. I genuinely believed I was now in the safe zone. Ann had moved on. She had decided that I'd been through enough and was ruining someone else's life. It seems that even if Ann *has* gone, she'll never truly be forgotten...

FALLING DOWN IS A PART OF LIFE.

CHOOSING TO GET BACK UP AGAIN IS LIVING...

Chapter 14

Setting out the circle of chairs, I take a moment to enjoy the silence and inhale deeply. As usual, I made it to the support group a short while before the meeting is due to start and I'm using my time wisely.

Unlike some other counsellors, my counselling style is very casual and unrestricted, but there's one thing I insist on. Before I chair a meeting, I have to take a moment to clear my mind and put my own problems to one side. I quickly discovered that I can't fully commit to the role if my mind is constantly wandering to other issues. Over time, I've learned to leave my own troubles at the door and pick them back up again on the way back out.

After my woodland adventures yesterday, Mateo and I spent the evening trying to wind down. Whilst I scribbled away in my diary, Mateo took great delight in ripping holes in the new sofa throw. Despite being on this planet for twenty-six years, I've only recently started a diary. Putting my feelings down on paper was Ruby's idea and despite my initial reservations, I must admit that I find it strangely addictive. Yes, there are weeks that go by where I don't give it a second thought, but once I pick it up, I find it difficult to put back down again. Writing down those niggling thoughts is proving to be the only way to get rid of them.

It's surprising how many thoughts run through your mind on a daily basis. Ninety percent of which you forget five seconds later. At first, I didn't really know what to write. I've always thought diaries were for hormonal teenagers and unorganised women in the midst of a mid-life crisis, but after a slow start, I've got it down to a fine art.

Placing the final chair in the centre of the circle, I look up to see Aidan stepping into the room.

'Hey!' I look down at my watch and realise there are still fifteen minutes to go. 'You're early...'

Since his visit to Blossom View, I haven't seen or heard from him, but I was secretly hoping he would reappear at Anxiety Anonymous. We came so close to making progress a couple of days back, it would be such a shame for him to abandon counselling before we have even started.

'I wanted to catch you before the others arrived.' Dropping his backpack onto one of the chairs, he rifles through it before producing a sleek business card. 'I called around a few places regarding your damp and these guys come highly recommended. They're competitively priced and can start the work whenever you're ready.'

'That's so nice of you, Aidan. Thank you.' Touched by his kind gesture, I take the card and smile gratefully. 'You didn't have to do that...'

I trail off as I notice a couple of paintbrushes sticking out of his backpack. 'Are those brushes?' I ask, leaning over for a closer look.

Nodding in response, Aidan opens the bag to reveal a selection of brushes, rollers and paint samples. 'I was thinking over what you said at the last meeting, about keeping busy?'

Happy that he's acted on my advice, I nod along and beam brightly.

'I have a lot of spare time on my hands and it enables me to overthink things. So, to stop me from going crazy, I thought I could help you with the decorating. That is, if you don't mind?'

'That's a great idea, but are you sure there isn't anything else you would rather be doing? I'm not sure there are many people who would give up their free time to paint someone else's walls.'

Aidan smiles and shrugs his shoulders. 'Well, I'm not sure there are many other people with a mind like mine...'

I hold his gaze for a moment, searching for the right thing to say. In the end, I choose to breeze straight past it.

'How are you fixed for tomorrow?' I ask, as a couple of people arrive for the meeting and promptly take their seats.

Aidan nods in agreement and I excuse myself to chair the meeting, just as Ruby walks into the room.

'Hi!' I say in confusion. 'What are you doing here? Shouldn't you be at work?'

'I got off early, so I thought I would come along.' Blowing a bubble with her chewing gum, she scans the seating area and whispers in my ear. 'Why does that guy look so familiar?'

Already knowing she is talking about Aidan, I don't bother to turn around.

'Is that who you were talking to in the street the other day?' She presses, keeping her eyes fixed on him.

'Yes.' Not wanting to draw unwanted attention to Aidan, I turn my back to him. 'He's staying at the B&B opposite the farm, so you might recognise him from there.'

'The Shepard?' Ruby asks sceptically, screwing up her button nose. 'He's staying at Leonard's place? Why?'

'You tell me.' I reply, organising the stack of paperwork on my desk. 'It's hardly luxury, is it? I was worried it was going to fall down and take me with it.'

'I'm surprised health and safety haven't condemned the place. My dad has been telling Leonard to sell up for years now.' She bites her lip and steals a discreet glimpse at Aidan. 'Wait a minute, why were you at The Shepard?'

'I happened to see him when I was at your mum's party. He invited me over...' As soon as the words escape my lips, I silently kick myself. 'Anyway, you should sit down, we're about to start.'

'Hold your horses!' Ruby exclaims, her eyes wide with curiosity. 'Do you care to elaborate on that?'

'Not right now.' I hiss, very aware of the many pairs of eyes that are burning into us. 'We can talk later...'

* * *

'So, he's been *here*, too?' Ruby demands, looking at me as though I have completely lost my mind. 'Why?'

'Like I said, he was giving me building advice.' Ruby's eyes narrow and I try my best to sound nonchalant. 'Honestly, there's nothing more to it.'

'You couldn't find another builder?' Clearly not willing to accept my explanation, Ruby continues to give me the third degree. 'One from the area who could actually carry out the work?'

'You sound like Aldo.' I grumble, pushing myself up from the grass and dusting mud from my jeans. 'Speaking of which, he should be here at any moment.'

Heading into the kitchen, I groan as I hear Ruby running inside after me.

'I understand you're just trying to help this guy, but don't feel like you're obliged to, you know, *befriend* people...'

'You befriended me and look how well that turned out.' I reply, shooting her a wink.

Not being able to deny this, Ruby reluctantly nods in agreement. 'Just don't get too involved and make *his* problems *your* problems.'

'Point taken.' Grabbing a cloth, I wipe down the work surfaces and fill the sink with soapy water. 'Anyway, that's enough about Aidan. How are you?'

A look of worry flashes across Ruby's face, immediately signalling a red flag.

'I'm fine.' She insists, hopping onto the kitchen counter and pretending to be completely absorbed in the spice rack.

'Fine?' I repeat doubtfully, not believing this for a second. 'What is it? Come on, spit it out.'

Choosing to ignore me, she picks up a bottle of basil and inspects the label closely.

'Is it Escapism?'

'No! I love Escapism. You know how much my job means to me.' Ruby squirms, visibly wanting the ground to swallow her up, but I continue to stare at her regardless.

'Then what is it?' I probe, keeping my gaze fixed on her.

Pressing her for information when she clearly doesn't want to give it up might seem harsh, but if something is bothering her, I want to hear about it.

'Frank.' She eventually mumbles, turning her attention to Mateo. 'It's probably nothing, but I've felt a little... *uneasy* lately.'

My heart tightens at the mention of Frank. 'Oh, Ruby...'

'It's no big deal.' She protests. 'Coming along to the meetings has helped me to keep him at bay.'

'Why didn't you say anything?' I ask softly, genuinely upset that she hasn't confided in me.

'Because it's ridiculous!' She exclaims, folding her arms crossly. 'I've been so annoyed with myself. For the first time in my life, things are going really well and I'm just waiting for it to fall apart. I'm constantly testing myself, because I genuinely can't believe my luck. It's got to the stage where I'm worrying, because I'm *not* worrying.'

'I'm so sorry you're feeling low.' Reaching out, I give her arm a gentle squeeze. 'It's a horrible thing to accept, but anxiety isn't something you can turn off and walk away from. You're the one who taught me that, remember?'

Managing a tiny nod, Ruby mumbles in agreement and picks up Mateo.

'Unfortunately, anxiety doesn't care whether things are good or bad. Frank isn't fussy. He will bulldoze his way into your life either way. You just have to be strong enough to know that *you're* the one in control.'

Ruby reluctantly smiles and strokes Mateo's cheek.

'Have you spoken to your mum about it?' I ask, reaching into the drawer and handing her a bag of cat treats.

'My mum is the *last* person I want to talk to when Frank comes knocking.' She sighs heavily and wipes her hands on a tea towel. 'Even after all these years, she still doesn't get it. The last time I mentioned Frank to her, she got really mad and told me this has gone on for long enough. Sometimes, I think she resents me for it.'

'Resents you? Why on earth would she resent you?'

'The time and money they have put into fixing me, I guess.' She shrugs her shoulders sadly. 'I thought I was making progress by taking the internship, but maybe I haven't. Maybe I am just pretending. Maybe I am acting out a role that isn't real...'

'Am *I* pretending?' I fire back, consumed with annoyance at her mother's attitude to her obvious torment. 'Am *I* acting out a role that isn't real?'

'Of course not!' Ruby frowns and takes a sip of water. 'You're doing amazingly well. You have taken a bad experience and turned it into something literally life-changing. You're my hero.'

Tears prick at the corners of my eyes and I desperately blink them back. Before I can reply, Mateo *meows* as Aldo appears in the back garden.

'Batman.' He says decidedly, walking into the kitchen with two pizza boxes. 'Batman is my hero, hands down.'

I exchange confused glances with Ruby and wait for him to explain himself.

'Oh, come on!' Aldo protests, flipping open the lid and taking a huge slice. 'He's totally the coolest superhero!'

'Why?' Ruby asks, reaching into the box and suppressing a giggle.

'He's just a man!' He exclaims, grabbing a bottle of wine from the fridge. 'Nothing unbelievable, no gimmicks and no stupid costumes...'

Not knowing which one of those three to debunk first, I accept a slice of pizza and chew away happily. Laughter fills the kitchen as Aldo and Ruby tease one another playfully. Anyone can be a superhero. It's not always about having a cape or supernatural powers. The real heroes are all around us. They slip in and out of our lives without us even knowing and if we're really lucky, they decide to stick around for a little while...

Chapter 15

'What do you think of this for the front door?' I ask, pointing to a burgundy tab on the colour wheel.

Reaching for the paint sample, Aidan shoots me a questioning look and raises his eyebrows. 'It's your house. It's your call.'

'Okay...' Swallowing a giggle, I stand back to scour the other options. 'What would *you* go for?'

Taking a moment to assess the rainbow of colours, he points to a turquoise tab confidently. 'This one.'

Not being convinced, I hold the sample close to my face. *Blue Boulevard*. I wouldn't have bothered to give this shade a second look, but now that I have it in my hands, I don't want to put it down. The blue has a unique grey undertone, making it both charming and sophisticated. There's something almost celestial and captivating about it.

'Let's go for it.' I announce, slipping the card back into its resting place on the display.

'Don't you want to take a few samples to try it out first?' Aidan asks, his hand hovering over the pots of paint.

'No, I trust you.' Taking hold of our shopping trolley, I wait for him to grab a giant tub and dump it amongst the mountain of masking tape and dust sheets.

As we make our way to the cashier, I marvel at just how well this morning has gone. When Aidan arrived at Blossom View earlier, we jumped straight into the car to hit the DIY store. I was a little concerned that traipsing around the shops with a near stranger would be a tad awkward, but Aidan has been surprisingly cheerful. We haven't discussed the support group, his past or his mental health, but Aidan seems to be more at ease than I've ever seen him. It just shows that sometimes, a little normality can be all the therapy a person needs.

Once we have paid and buckled ourselves into our seats, I flick on the radio as we head back to the cottage. Cruising along the road, we fall into a comfortable silence as music drifts out of the speakers. I look over at Aidan and smile as I notice him silently singing along to the music. Catching me looking at him, he swiftly stops humming and clears his throat.

'She used to love this song.' He mumbles, scratching his stubble and pulling his brow into a frown.

'Who did?' I ask, turning it up for him to enjoy.

'My wife...'

Sensing that I've touched upon a delicate subject, I discreetly turn the volume back down.

'We would sing this in the car as we drove along the beach. I can still hear her voice now, as though she's right here with me. That vision of us tearing along the road is what haunts me every night. Every single time I close my eyes she's there and I'm right back in that moment. Reliving it over and over again...'

Gripping the steering wheel tightly, I indicate right and swing around the roundabout, trying my best not to appear shocked by what he is telling me.

'Every emotion I felt at that moment comes flooding back to me on a nightly basis, until I finally block it out enough to grab a few hours of sleep. The anguish of realising she's not next to me in the morning is ten times worse than the agony of the night before.'

Completely lost for words, sadness fills my heart as the song comes to an end and dance music takes its place. Turning onto the driveway, I bring the car to a steady stop and pull on the handbrake, racking my brains for the right thing to say.

Immediately snapping out of it, Aidan grabs the bags from his feet and reaches for the handle. 'Alright, let's get to work on this door.'

Smiling back at him, I tactfully drop the subject and lead the way inside. As Aidan tears open the packaging on his paintbrushes, I wander into the garden in search of Mateo. Just as I left him an hour ago, he's sprawled out on the grass, joyfully basking in the sunshine.

Propping open the door to allow the breeze to blow through the cottage, I frown at the faded paintwork.

'Aidan...' I shout, peering closely at the old back door. 'Do you think we have enough paint to do this door as well?'

Stepping into the garden, Aidan runs his fingers over the wood and nods. 'We have more than enough, but I should probably start with this one as it will need sanding down first.'

'Fab!' I twist my hair into a ponytail and pull a pair of gardening overalls from the pantry.

Stepping into the scratchy onesie, I reach for the strange ball of barbed wire he is holding. 'What do I do with this?'

'It's to remove the remnants of the old coat before we apply the new paint.' He explains, handing me a pair of gloves.

'Like nail polish?' I ask, copying his movement and making circular motions on the panelling.

'I'm sorry?'

'Never mind.' I mumble. Sometimes, I forget that not all men are manicure-loving extroverts like Aldo.

'Actually, you're right.' Aidan says suddenly. 'It's *exactly* like nail polish. If you think of it in manicure terms, we're stripping the nail back to its natural state before applying the base coat.'

'I thought as much!' I let out a laugh and press the scouring pad against the wood.

'My wife was a beautician.' He adds, explaining his knowledge of women's beauty treatments.

Realising this is the second time he's spoken about his wife, I decide to try and explore the subject further. I've established that his wife is central to his torment, but I still have absolutely no idea why. All I have are random scraps of information that I'm trying to piece together like a complex jigsaw.

'What's her name?' I ask, making an effort to keep my voice light.

'It's Melanie.' Aidan sighs and I notice his shoulders tense up. 'Or at least, it *was* Melanie.'

Hearing the confirmation that Aidan's wife has sadly passed away makes my heart break for him.

'Well, Mel, not Melanie. She hated being called Melanie. Only her mother got away with calling her that.' Aidan grins and for the first time since I met him, his eyes crinkle into the smile. 'It's impossible to comprehend that she isn't around anymore...'

'I'm so sorry.' I reply, my heart physically hurting for his loss.

Wiping the old paint fragments to the floor, he kneels down to scour the bottom of the panel. 'Mel was my first love. We met on the first day of college and never looked back. I always thought I was incredibly lucky to have made it through life without having my heart broken, but now I'm paying the ultimate price.' Looking down at his bare ring finger, he raises his eyebrows sadly. 'Have *you* ever had your heart broken?'

'Once.' I reply, reaching up to the top of the door. 'There's nothing quite like the pain of being hurt by someone you love. That empty ache inside you just won't leave. It's like grief.' I stop to wipe my brow and realise he's staring at me. 'My failed engagement is actually how I found myself at Anxiety Anonymous.'

I automatically glance down at the infamous inking on my finger and feel a plethora of emotions hit my stomach.

'How did you transfer from attending to hosting?' He asks, dropping his scouring pad as Mateo jumps into his lap.

'It's a long story.'

'Well, I've got a lot of time...'

Chapter 16

The sun set hours ago, yet Aidan is still here. He is still painting and we are still talking. I haven't got to the bottom of exactly what happened to Mel and I'm a little afraid to ask. The snippets of information he's revealing are painting the world's saddest picture. What happened to Aidan's wife and how did it lead to him being in the middle of the Cheshire countryside, hundreds of miles away from home?

'We agreed on everything from politics to religion, but music divided us each and every time.' He laughs gently and dips his brush into a tin of white paint, before carefully running it along the skirting board. 'She would have loved it up here. Cheshire is very similar to Surrey.'

I crouch down to apply masking tape to the floorboards and smile. 'What is your home life like?'

Aidan pauses and wipes a blob of paint from his forearm. 'We had a lovely semi-detached, just outside of London. Mel adored that place, but it's gone now. I don't have a home anymore.'

'You must have a home.' I reply, tearing off the end of the tape with my teeth. 'Even if that home is only temporary.'

He exhales loudly and taps his brush against the paint pot. 'In that case, I guess The Shepard is my home.'

'How long do you plan on staying there?' Folding my legs beneath me, I lean across him and remove a smear of magnolia from the floor.

'I haven't really thought about it, but it's where I shall be until I figure out my next move.' He says decidedly, resting the brush on a pile of newspaper.

Watching Mateo pad over the rug in his search for a suitable resting spot, I take a moment to admire the fresh paintwork. 'What are your options?'

'The world is my oyster, but I don't want to be a part of it without Mel.' He mumbles sadly, moving further along the skirting board. 'I don't want to be *anywhere* anymore. The only place I want to be is with my wife.'

Sensing that he's becoming uncomfortable with my questions, I clap my hands together and jump to my feet. 'You must be starving after all the work you have done today. The least I can do is repay you with a meal. What do you say?'

Aidan inspects the skirting board for a final time before sealing the tin of paint. 'It's very kind of you to offer, but I should probably be heading back to the B&B. It's getting pretty late.'

I look down at my watch and I'm surprised to discover it's almost midnight. I would say that time flies when you're having fun, but tonight hasn't exactly been fun. It's been sad, heart-breaking and utterly absorbing, but to call it *fun* would be incredibly insensitive.

'I can't believe it's so late!' I stammer, slightly embarrassed. 'I'm terribly sorry for keeping you.'

'It's fine.' Aidan dismisses my apologies and pushes himself to his feet. 'It's been nice to talk to someone instead of driving myself crazy at The Shepard.'

I smile happily, overjoyed that he's seeing the benefits of talking about his feelings. 'Now that you've seen how liberating it is to talk about your emotions instead of keeping them bottled up, maybe you will feel comfortable enough to speak at the support group?'

'I don't know.' His smile freezes and he shakes his head reluctantly. 'You're a lot easier to talk to than a room of strangers.'

Blood rushes to my face as I start to clear away the newspaper. 'Why?'

'Because you don't ask me any questions that I don't want to answer.' Reaching for his jacket, he gives Mateo a final stroke of the head. 'What time is the last bus back to Mobberley?'

Automatically reaching for my car keys, I shrug my shoulders. 'I have no idea, but I'll give you a lift home. It's the least I can do.'

'Are you sure?' He asks, tugging on his backpack.

'Like I said, it's the least I can do.'

Slipping on my trainers, I head out to the car and wait for Aidan to fasten his seatbelt before pulling out onto the quiet lane.

'You know, there's a taxi service if you want to get around, rather than relying on public transport.' I change gear as we breeze past the deserted golf course. 'That bus route is unreliable at the best of times.'

'Taxi drivers want to chat. They want to know all about your day. The good, not the bad. I can't lie for the sake of small talk.' Aidan replies, turning to look out of the window. 'The bus, on the other hand, is always quiet. No one talks to me, no one looks at me, no one even breathes in my direction.'

Slowing down as we approach a sharp corner, I resist the urge to remind him once again that talking is exactly what he needs.

'Did *you* find it hard to talk to people?' He asks, placing his elbow on the armrest. 'It seems to come so naturally to you.'

'I can assure you, it doesn't. Even after all this time, talking about my feelings can still be uncomfortable and that's completely normal. From being young children, it's drilled into us that we shouldn't talk to strangers. We are constantly reminded to not reveal anything about ourselves to people we don't know.'

Aidan nods along, seemingly absorbed in what I am saying. 'I can actually remember my mother saying something similar.'

'Exactly. To reveal our innermost fears to strangers goes against everything we have ever known to be normal, which is why we find it so difficult.' We come to a stop at a set of lights and I turn to face Aidan. 'But it does get easier. Just as quickly as we taught ourselves to keep things buried, we can teach ourselves to open up.'

The lights change to amber and I lift my foot off the brake.

'You make it sound so easy.' He groans, as I hit the accelerator.

'I never said it would be easy. What I am saying is that it's possible and that's where faith comes into it. If you have faith, absolutely *everything* is possible.' I turn left onto a country road and flick on the high beams. 'We must always have two things in life. Faith and hope. Hope is having the ability to hear the music of the future and faith is having the courage to dance to it today.'

Looking over at Aidan, I can't help noticing he looks like he's seen a ghost.

'Are you okay?' I ask cautiously, debating whether I should pull over.

Quickly composing himself, Aidan looks down at his lap. 'I'm fine. It's just, Mel used to say those exact words to me.'

A strange feeling washes over me as I stare at the road ahead.

'As long as I have hope, faith, a bed beneath me and the stars above me, all will be right with the world.' He smiles fondly and holds his ring finger to his lips. 'How did it come to this?'

My mouth becomes inexplicably dry as I search for the right answer to his question. What do you say to someone who has tragically lost their wife, ran away from home and confided in you, a complete stranger, over everyone else? Not even the extensive counselling courses teach you how to deal with this.

'You don't think it will ever happen to you, do you?' He ponders, tapping his room key on his knee. 'The number of road accidents I used to see driving back and forth down the motorway. I'd give them a cursory glance and continue with my journey. I didn't really think about them after that. I wouldn't give another thought to the fact that someone's life had just changed forever.'

Road accidents? Did Mel die in a car crash?

'Don't ever take people for granted, Sadie. Tell those you care about you love them, because tomorrow isn't promised to anyone. My dad used to tell me that, but I didn't take any notice until it was too late.'

I smile sadly in response and rest my hand on the gearstick. My heart is breaking for him, but I refuse to let him see. Aidan's a proud man. Sympathy will only cause him to clam up again.

I try to focus on my driving, but my mind is brooding over Aidan's words. It's no secret my own mother and I don't get along, but I would be devastated if anything happened to her. I try to picture myself telling her I love her. Three little words neither of us has said in many years.

'Are you close with your parents?' He asks, as though reading my mind.

'No.' I answer honestly. 'My mum and I have a somewhat strained relationship and I've never met my dad.' Even though this has been the case all of my life, saying it out loud still stings.

'How about you?' I ask, turning the tables on him. 'Are you close with your parents?'

'I idolised my mother, but she passed away a few years back. My dad is back in Surrey. He lives with my sister and her family...' Spotting The Shepard in the near distance, Aidan falls into silence.

We pass Ruby's farm and I notice that apart from one light, the entire building is in darkness. Knowing that Ruby spends her evenings watching YouTube clips of different holiday resorts across the globe, I smile to myself and swing into the B&B's car park.

'Thank you so much for today.' Flicking on the interior light, I turn down the radio. 'You're a star.'

'It was my pleasure.' He replies quietly. 'To be honest, I had started to forget what human interaction was like. A bit of normality is exactly what I needed.'

My heart swells with pride at the difference in Aidan. He is a million miles away from the sullen man who crawled into Anxiety Anonymous just over a week ago. Despite Aldo's reservations, I knew all he needed was a friendly chat and the willing ear of someone who would listen.

'Well, whenever you want to feel *normal* there's a whole cottage back there just crying out for a someone to bring it back to life.'

'Ironically, that is exactly what today has done for me.' Aidan releases the handle and steps out of the car. 'Thank you, Sadie.'

I smile back at him and nod as he quietly closes the door and walks over the gravel towards the entrance. Immediately starting the engine, I put the car into reverse and spin around, before turning back onto the empty road. As I press my foot to the floor, I glimpse into the rear-view mirror and notice Aidan watching my car disappear into the darkness. Sadness weighs heavy on my shoulders at leaving him here alone. He's a grieving man, miles away from home, in a frankly desolate bed and breakfast. He should be being comforted by his friends and family, not detaching himself from those who love him.

I've always believed that having faith is being able to see the light with your heart, when all your eyes can see is darkness. Anxiety and depression create mountains that seem impossible to climb, but with faith and hope, we *can* move them...

Chapter 17

Stirring my spoon around the giant mug, I get comfortable in the plush armchair and watch a busker playing his guitar across the street. I've been waiting for Julia in Thelma's Tea Room for around fifteen minutes, but I should clarify that the delay isn't Julia's fault, it's mine. Generally, punctuality isn't something I'm known for, but when it comes to Thelma's Tea Room, I could arrive an hour early and *still* wish I'd come earlier. With its shabby-chic interior and resident Poodle, Thelma, Thelma's Tea Room is unique in its retro charm. You could sit here for hours and still find something new to look at.

The sound of the door chime twinkling brings me back to reality, just in time to see Julia striding across the café towards me. As usual, her bohemian-inspired fashion sense is in full swing and her bangles jangle together loudly as she shakes off her vintage jacket.

'Sadie!' She gushes, planting a red kiss on both of my cheeks. 'How are you?'

Quickly grabbing the attention of the waiter, I order Julia a cappuccino as she takes her seat.

'I'm good. How are you?' I reply, my smile widening as I take in her deep tan. 'How was Portugal?'

'Fabulous, but more importantly, how are things at Anxiety Anonymous?' Julia rolls up her sleeves and pushes her glasses into her grey curls.

'Great. My release cushion idea has been very well received.' I pause as another mug appears on the table. 'Admittedly, people were a little sceptical at first, but I asked around at the last meeting and they're keen to keep it.'

'Excellent!' Julia raises the cup to her lips and places it back down when she realises it's too hot to drink. 'Maybe I should run the idea past the charity. It might be a good idea to roll it out across all branches.'

My lips stretch into a smile at the thought of my idea being implemented up and down the country.

'And how are you within yourself?' Julia asks suddenly, making me squirm in my seat.

'Like I said earlier, I'm good.' I flash her my most reassuring smile and pick up the menu.

Being a counsellor herself and effectively my boss, Julia has this knack of knowing when I'm holding something back.

'No bad days you want to talk about?' She presses, slipping on her glasses and narrowing her eyes.

My mind flits back to my panic in the woods and I feel my skin prickle. Convincing myself it's not worth mentioning, I decide to leave it out.

'Honestly, I'm fine!' I laugh off her concerns and push the menu towards her.

Seemingly unconvinced, she takes the menu and flips through the laminated pages. 'How did the house move go?'

'Pretty smoothly, but the cottage requires quite a bit of building work...'

'I can recommend a few people.' Diving into her handbag, she pulls out a floral address book. 'In fact, my brother-in-law is...'

'I've already hired someone, but thank you so much.' I rest my elbows on the table, weighing up whether or not I should tell her about Aidan. 'It's actually someone from the support group.'

Julia kicks her tote bag beneath the table and beams brightly. 'That's great! At least you'll know where to find him if you're not happy with the work!'

I laugh along and feel myself start to relax. I knew Aldo and Ruby were making a mountain out of a molehill. If Julia thought for a second that it was inappropriate to hire Aidan, she wouldn't hold back in voicing her concerns. Trying to defeat the opinion that sufferers of anxiety and depression should be treated with an air of caution is one of my main objectives at the support group. Normality is what they crave and my job is to ensure normality is exactly what they will get...

* * *

Waving goodbye to Julia, I weave through the blanket of people and come to a stop outside an old antique store. A dazzling presentation of vintage rubies and seductive emeralds sparkle back at me as my inner shopaholic screams out for a jewel. The lure of a gem to slip onto my finger and lose myself in its magic has me itching for my bank card.

Just as I am tearing myself away from the stunning display, my stomach drops as I see a figure I recognise inside the shop. A quick double-take confirms to me that the shadowy silhouette belongs to my mother. Watching her wander around the store, I debate making a swift escape, but my feet feel frozen to the spot. Exchanging her card for a glossy bag, she raps her nails on the counter as the cashier passes her a lengthy receipt.

An almost trance-like state takes over me as she pushes her way out onto the street.

'Sadie!' She exclaims, stopping abruptly and dusting down her blazer. 'What are you doing here?'

'Hi, Mum.' Tucking my hair behind my ears, I immediately feel self-conscious. How does she do that? How does she manage to make me feel an inch tall within seconds of being in her presence?

'What are you doing here?' She repeats, clearly not impressed at bumping into me.

'I met a friend for lunch.' I reply, choosing not to tell her about Julia given her disdain for my choice of career. 'How are you?'

'Fabulous.' She shakes her chocolate bob and her earrings twinkle gently. 'I'm just picking up some things for our trip to New York next week.'

My eyes flit to the antique store behind her and back again. Realising she isn't going to ask how I am, I decide to move the conversation along.

'So, I moved into Blossom View.' I stand to the left to allow a group of shoppers to pass. 'It's finally starting to feel like home.'

'Uh huh...' She mumbles, obviously still no happier at my decision to purchase the cottage.

'It's perfect. Mateo loves it, too.'

She looks at me blankly and I bite my lip.

'The cat, Mum. Remember?'

'Of course!' She exclaims, forcing a thin smile. 'The cat.'

We stand opposite one another in the street, neither of us knowing what to say. Recognising that if we have any hope of building a relationship I have to be the bigger person and step up, I clear my throat awkwardly.

'I don't suppose you want to grab a coffee, do you?' I point to the cafe opposite and bite my lip as she stares back at me, completely stumped.

'I would love to, but I'm meeting Mick for dinner shortly and I don't want to be late.' She stammers, frantically looking at her watch for effect. 'You know how he is.'

A smile twitches at the corner of my mouth and I don't know whether I want to laugh or cry. My mother's partner is a sore subject at the best of times and today is no different.

'You're welcome to join us...' She adds hastily. 'We're going for a drink with a few of his friends first.' Her eyes dart around nervously, begging me to decline and be on my way.

'Thanks, but I should probably get going.'

She visibly breathes a sigh of relief and smooths down her hair. Mick will always be her priority and that will never change. She will continue to detach herself from everyone around her, just to keep her horrid Mick smiling.

'Well, it's good to see you, Sadie. I hope all these *changes* you've made are making you happy.' She gabbles, trying to put meaning behind her words.

If this strained conversation wasn't so uncomfortable, I would actually laugh out loud. Only my mother would see leaving stilettoes and a materialistic life behind as a negative thing.

'I *am* happy.' I insist, suddenly very aware that we're having this chat in the middle of a very busy street.

Studying my mother's face, I notice her twitching awkwardly.

'I better get going.' She announces, taking a step back and pointing in the opposite direction to which we are facing. 'We shall have to go for that coffee another time.'

'Definitely.' I confirm, both of us safe in the knowledge that this arrangement won't take place.

Tugging down her sleeves, she smiles thinly and starts to walk away, the sound of her heels clacking loudly on the pavement echoing in her wake. As I watch her weave through the sea of shoppers, Aidan's words ring loudly in my ears.

Don't ever take anyone for granted, Sadie.
Tell those you care about you love them, because
tomorrow isn't promised to anyone.

'Mum!' I yell, the words firing out of my mouth before I can stop them.

Racing after her, I don't stop running until we are just a few feet apart.

'I love you...' I whisper, not quite believing what I'm saying.

'I'm sorry?' Screwing up her nose, she leans in closer and frowns.

'I *love* you.' I repeat, my skin flushing violently as a passer-by shoots me a strange look.

'Are you okay?' She asks, obviously perturbed by my unusual public declaration.

The look of complete and utter shock on her face is enough to make me giggle. 'I'm fine! I just wanted you to know that I love you!'

'Well, that's very... *nice*.' Fidgeting uneasily, she casts a look around to ensure no one is listening. 'I love you, too.'

A laugh escapes my lips as she makes a fast escape and vanishes into the crowd. My mother and I haven't exchanged those three little words in so long, I actually can't remember the last time they were said. Hearing her say it now, regardless of how strained and forced it was, lifted my spirits immensely.

She might ridicule my decision to become a counsellor, but she has unwittingly just been counselled and she doesn't even know it...

Chapter 18

Checking my phone for messages, I try to ignore the niggling feeling in my stomach that something is wrong. I've just wrapped up the latest Anxiety Anonymous meeting and it's troubling me greatly that Aidan didn't show. Of course, he has no obligation to attend, but the little voice in the back of my mind is telling me that something isn't quite right.

After our decorating marathon, I had high hopes that Aidan had turned a corner. He divulged more to me in that one day than the whole time he has been at the meetings. I look down at my phone and tap my fingers on the screen. I don't have any way of contacting him and I think rocking up at The Shepard to check on him would be crossing the line into obsessive.

Convincing myself he will come to tomorrow's meeting, I slip my phone into my bag and push my way outside.

'Shirley!' A deep voice yells in the distance.

Looking over my shoulder, I break into a smile as I see Aldo striding towards me.

'What are you doing here?' I ask, offering him my cheek for a kiss.

He waves a bottle of fizz in the air and slips his leather-clad arm through mine. 'Fancy a drink?'

Resting my head on his shoulder, I let him lead me towards his car. 'You have no idea how good that sounds.'

Climbing into Aldo's Audi, I study his pretty face and immediately reminisce about days gone by. For many years, Aldo and I were inseparable and I wouldn't have had it any other way.

'Why can't we just stay young forever?' I muse, clicking in my seatbelt as Aldo turns over the engine. 'Life was so much easier back then.'

'Was it really though?' He glances in his mirror before pulling onto the road. 'The easy option is to look back through rose-tinted glasses...'

I turn to face him and shoot him a questioning look. Is Aldo right? Is the time I look back on so fondly not as sweet as it once seemed?

'Just think about it. Back then, our only concern was for cigarettes and alcohol. It was fun while it lasted, but if we're honest, it was an empty existence.'

'Cigarettes?' I repeat, not being very impressed with him dismissing that time of our lives as hollow. 'I never smoked!'

Aldo laughs at my reaction and squeezes my knee reassuringly. 'Oh, come on. You know what I mean! We have both moved on since then. We've grown-up. We finally care about people other than ourselves.'

'I've always cared about you!' I interrupt in annoyance, slapping away his hand.

'One another, aside.' He adds, drumming his fingers on the steering wheel. 'We've joined the real world and on the whole, it's pretty great.'

I cast my mind over the last six months and nod in response. 'I guess you're right, but those years were some of the best times of my life...'

I trail off as I realise Aldo is pulling over opposite the apartment block where we used to live. Putting down his window, he strains his neck and looks up at the iconic building. You can't see much from down here, but it doesn't stop the memories flooding back, both good and horrendously bad.

'You know I come past here every day, don't you?' I whisper, weirdly feeling as though I need to keep my voice down in case the apartment overhears.

'So do I...' Aldo mumbles. 'But it's not the same as actually taking a moment to soak it up. We should go back in and have a look around.'

My blood runs cold and I shake my head. 'Why would you want to do that?'

'Just to reminisce.' He lets out a yearning sigh and points at our old window. 'This place still feels like home to me.'

'The apartment is in the past.' I attempt to smile at him, but my frown stays firmly in place. 'If you keep looking back, you'll never fully move on.'

'Don't be a party pooper!' He teases, putting the window back up and turning off the engine. 'Let's go in...'

'No!' I yell, a little louder than I intended. 'Can we please just go home?'

Aldo squints at me suspiciously. 'What's going on, Shirley?'

'Nothing!' I force myself to smile and motion for him to put the car into gear. 'I'm fine.'

'No, you're not. You've got those shifty eyes you get when you're worried.'

Automatically closing my eyes so that he can't see them, I silently curse myself as I realise he's right. I *am* worried. I am worried about Aidan and as hard as

I'm trying to fight it, Aldo sees straight through my positive mask.

All throughout the meeting, I kept my focus fixed on the door, just waiting to breathe a sigh of relief as he walked through it. It's taking all of my willpower to not drive up to The Shepard and check on him. He's hundreds of miles away from home, he doesn't know where is and he doesn't have a single person he can lean on.

'Shirley...' Aldo nudges my leg and waves his arms around to regain my attention. 'What is it?'

Licking my dry lips, I let out a drained groan. 'I'm concerned about the welfare of one of the people at the support group.'

'Okay...' Aldo nods and scratches the tip of his nose. 'Isn't there some kind of process for that? Like a programme or a scheme you can refer her to?'

Deciding not to tell him that it's Aidan who I'm worried about, I take a deep breath before replying. 'Yes, but I just wish I could do more for them.'

Aldo smiles back at me proudly and starts the car. 'You really do put everything you have into your job, don't you? Most people shut off the second the clock strikes five.'

'It's not as simple as that when you're dealing with people...'

He indicates right and joins the steady stream of traffic. '*I* work with people and I shut off when I walk out of the door.'

'That's different.' I glance over my shoulder and watch our old apartment block disappear into the trees as we speed down the lane. 'You work with people's hair, not people's minds.'

Julia constantly reminds me that I can't allow my work at the support group to have a negative impact on my personal life and until now, I haven't. I know I am thinking about Aidan more than what is necessary, but no matter how hard I try, I just can't shake him from my mind. The thought of him in the B&B alone and grieving is tearing me up inside. He needs help, more help than he is receiving by attending the odd Anxiety Anonymous meeting.

Maybe he's decided that it's time to return to Surrey. Maybe he's taken the break that he needed and is now in the right frame of mind to start taking his life back. I picture him arriving in his hometown, surrounded by family members and friends who are delighted to have him in back in their circle.

Ruby's comment regarding the longevity of people in your life comes back to me and I chew over her words thoughtfully.

Not everyone is meant to stay in your life forever.

Aidan stumbling into my life like he did was so random and I will forever be grateful that our paths crossed, even if this is where our journey ends. After all, life doesn't give you the people you think you *want*. Life gives you the people you *need*. It gives you people to love, to hate, to make you, to break you and to transform you into the person you were always destined to be...

Chapter 19

My stomach throbs with laughter as I reach over and clink my glass against Aldo's.

'I know what we should do!' He suddenly exclaims, sitting bolt upright on the couch. 'Let's download a dating app!'

With a mouthful of bubbles, I resort to a firm shake of the head.

'Oh, come on! It will be fun!' Grabbing my phone from the coffee table, he starts to tap at the keypad as I furiously hit him with cushions. 'It just takes a few clicks...'

Before I can put down my fizz, Aldo's face breaks into a smile as he waves the handset around happily. Sliding across the sofa, Aldo taps the screen repeatedly. 'It's so easy. All you have to do is tap twice if you like the person and once if you don't. But first, I need a photo of you.'

'No!' I protest, covering my face with my hands as he bats them away playfully. 'How do *you* know how this works, anyway?'

'*Everyone* knows how this works.' Aldo shrugs his shoulders as his lip curls into a grin. 'Oh, here we go. I can just use your Facebook picture.'

Knowing that he isn't going to give up, I grab my glass and squint at the screen as he quickly fills in the registration details.

'Now, he's cute, right?' Aldo muses, delight beaming out of his face at being tasked with scouring through a catalogue of hot men. 'What do you think?'

Taking the phone from him, I look at the man staring back at me. It doesn't take me more than ten seconds to realise that he isn't for me. Tapping the picture, I wait for the next image to load.

'What was wrong with him?' Aldo asks, shuffling closer for a better look.

'He has a mohawk...' I grumble, swiping away the next image as soon as it loads.

'Oi!' He yells, snatching the phone out of my hands. 'There's no point if you're not going to play properly.'

Bringing up the previous image once more, he tilts the handset in my direction. 'How about this guy? He's hot!'

'He's also twenty-one!' I add, not succumbing to his razor-like cheekbones and chiselled jawline. 'Next...'

Aldo lets out an annoyed huff and takes a slug of his bubbles. As he skims through the pictures, I shake my head repeatedly. What's wrong with me? I'm being offered dozens of gorgeous men and I don't have so much as a twinge of interest.

Finally getting the hint, Aldo hands me back my phone before reaching into his pocket and producing his own. After scrolling through the images, he clears his throat dramatically and spins around the screen. Without breathing a word, he sits back and cradles his glass smugly.

Now we're talking. The man in the photo is undeniably beautiful. Wearing a slick black suit and a pair of thick-rimmed glasses, he stares confidently into the lens. His dark floppy hair is combed back neatly as his piercing eyes sparkle like chocolate diamonds against his olive skin.

'Well?' Aldo demands, already knowing what I'm about to say.

'He's alright.' I reply, making sure to get another glimpse of the hunk before handing over the phone. 'Who is it?'

'That, Shirley, is the guy I've been telling you about.' Aldo taps the screen and brings up another bunch of equally beautiful photos.

I stare at the handset in awe, not being able to deny that the man in the images is achingly attractive.

'His name is Pierce Harrington...' Aldo whispers, swooning over the photos himself. 'And he is desperate to meet you.'

'I am *honoured*.' I tease, taking a sip of fizz and snuggling into the cushions.

'So, you'll go?' Aldo confirms, fist pumping the air in celebration.

'No.' I mumble, bracing myself for an attack.

He stares at me open-mouthed, trying to work out if I'm joking. 'No?' He repeats finally. 'What the hell are you talking about? Why not?'

'Because there's no point. I'm not looking for a relationship at the moment, so I would just be wasting his time.' I hold out my glass for a refill as Aldo grabs the bottle from the cooler.

'You don't need to *marry* him!' He exclaims, filling my glass to the brim. 'It's not about putting a ring on it. It's about getting you back out there again.'

I stare down into my glass and watch the bubbles swim to the top like fireworks.

'I know this is out of your comfort zone, Shirley, but the magic only happens when you leave your bubble.' Aldo stretches out his skinny legs and brings up Pierce's picture once more. 'You're frightened. You're afraid of getting your heart hurt again, but if you don't go, you will be letting your anxiety control a whole area of your life. Just think of the advice you dish out at the meetings. You're neglecting a part of your life that you should be enjoying to the max.'

I nod along, recognising that everything he's saying is one hundred percent correct. Isn't it time I practice what I preach and taste my own medicine? Mateo stirs in his sleep and yawns lazily. Could I make room in my heart for another person? Mateo jumps to his feet and meows loudly, as though indicating that I could.

'Alright.' I announce finally. 'I'll do it...'

'You will?' Aldo shrieks, clinking his champagne flute against mine to seal the deal.

'I will.' I confirm, not being able to resist smiling back at him. 'Being wined and dined again wasn't on my bucket list, but if it will shut you up, I shall give it a go.'

'You won't regret it, Shirley. I swear, he's perfect for you!' Aldo beams brightly and kicks off his boots. 'Whilst we are on the subject, what *is* on your bucket list?'

Before I can respond, he tears two pages from the magazines on the coffee table and hands one to me, along with a chewed pen.

'Let's write them down and we can make it our mission to tick them off, one by one.'

You know it's time to step away from the alcohol when Aldo starts making lists. Draining my glass, I remove the pen lid with my teeth and watch Aldo scribble away busily. He's obviously been thinking about this for quite a while. Pulling my bobble out of my hair, I let my blonde locks fall around my shoulders and rack my brains for what exactly it is I want to do before I die.

Clearly not having the same trouble, Aldo drops his pen with a flourish.

'Are you ready?' He asks, not waiting for a response before starting to ramble off his list. 'I want to spend a year in Paris, I *have* to meet Nicky Clarke, I need to see Gaga live...'

'You have been spending far too much time with Edward!' I throw back my head and giggle as Aldo continues to reveal his lifelong ambitions.

When he finally finishes, he hands over his piece of paper proudly. Reading the never-ending list for myself, I picture Aldo doing each and every one. There's not a single part of me that doubts he will achieve his goals, and in a fabulous fashion, too.

'Your turn.' He demands, holding out his hand for my own list. 'Hand it over.'

Reaching down to stroke Mateo, I bite my lip and stare at the two words I squiggled on the sheet of paper in front of me. Confident there's nothing else I want to add, I flick it towards Aldo. Blinking repeatedly, as he always does when he's sozzled, he checks the back of the paper twice for anything he might have missed.

'Be happy?' He says, scowling and putting down his glass. 'That's not a bloody bucket list!'

'A bucket list is a list of things you wish to accomplish before you die, isn't it?' I ask, lifting Mateo onto my lap and holding him close to my chest.

Reluctantly nodding in agreement, Aldo's lips stretch into a smile.

'Well, if at the end of my time on earth I can say that I have lived a happy life, I will have achieved absolutely everything I wanted to...'

Chapter 20

Watching the release cushion make its way around the room, I try not to feel disheartened. He's not here, again. We are only five minutes from the end of the meeting and Aidan hasn't shown. I always find it difficult when people leave Anxiety Anonymous as I become so attached to them, but my instincts are telling me this isn't a usual case. Something doesn't feel quite right, I just can't put my finger on what it is.

As I ponder the circumstances around Aidan's mysterious disappearance, the release cushion lands with a gentleman I don't recognise. Immediately sitting up straight, he turns the pillow over in his hands.

'Hello.' He mumbles, his face immediately flushing as everyone's gaze turns to him. 'I'm not here for myself. I'm here for my daughter. My wife and I are in the process of divorcing and she isn't taking it all that well.'

Coming back to earth with a thud, I snap to attention and zone in on his words.

'I don't mean to sound naïve, but I'm not sure if she's suffering from anxiety. I've spent hours on end scouring the web and anxiety is the one thing I keep coming back to. She's not really eating, she doesn't want to get out of her bed and I'll randomly find her crying for no apparent reason. Trying to get her to attend a social event of any kind is near impossible.

The only place she seems to be comfortable is at home.'

He pauses and studies the release cushion closely before speaking again.

'I don't want to cause offence, but this whole *mental health thing* is all very new to me. I'm very much of a *pour yourself a drink and pull yourself together* kind of guy. I just came here in the hope that you can help me to understand what she's going through.'

Having heard these concerns many times in the past, I understand this perfectly. 'I realise how difficult it must be for you to comprehend your daughter's struggles, but it is very common for children to suffer symptoms of anxiety and depression after a divorce. Recognising that something is wrong is the first step in getting your daughter the help that she needs...'

'Help?' He interjects, looking rather worried. 'What kind of help?'

'Don't be alarmed. *Help* can be something as simple as talking.' I offer him a friendly smile in the hope that he relaxes. 'Have you tried speaking to your daughter about how she feels?'

'No.' He replies sadly. 'Every time I bring it up, she seems to push me further away. I thought it would be best not to draw attention to it.'

'A lot of children in her position feel neglected and unloved when their parents decide to separate. Keeping an open and honest communication between you will help her to realise the divorce isn't going to affect the relationship you have. Sometimes, talking is all the help a person needs...'

I continue to tell him about the forum and a few others chip in with snippets of advice before I wrap up the meeting and make my way outside.

As I slowly wander across the car park, I raise my eyebrows as I spot Ruby leaning against the bonnet of my car.

'You couldn't give me a lift home, could you?' She asks, smiling sweetly and immediately climbing into the car, not bothering to wait for a response.

After throwing my handbag and jacket into the boot, I jump into the driver's seat and shoot Ruby a questioning look. 'Is everything okay?'

She nods for a moment, before shaking her head as we turn out of the car park. 'I'm not sure...'

'What is it?' I press, already on high alert after our talk the other day.

Ruby cracks her knuckles nervously and rubs her face. 'I have a dilemma.'

The word *dilemma* causes my stomach to flip as I change lanes. 'Okay...' I reply, bracing myself for what I am about to hear.

'They want me to go to the Caribbean.'

I frown and indicate left, relief washing over me at discovering it isn't something horrific. 'Who does?'

'Escapism. They're sending a bunch of newbies on a tour of their bestselling hotels to get a better idea of what we're selling.' She pauses to assess my reaction before continuing. 'In total, we would see six islands and visit twenty-one hotels. It's two months and all expenses are paid...'

'That's amazing!' I gush, not being able to contain my enthusiasm. 'You must be so excited!'

Ruby remains silent and I nudge her knee. 'You are excited, aren't you?'

'I don't know. I don't think I'm going to go...'

'Why on earth not?' I exclaim, completely flabbergasted. 'It's your dream to travel! This is an incredible opportunity for you! You *have* to go!'

'I'm afraid, Sadie!' Ruby's voice wobbles as she turns down the radio. 'I can only just manage my anxiety here, in Cheshire, with you, Aldo and my family around me. What would I do if Frank found me out there? I don't think I could cope.'

Trying to keep my focus on the road, I shake my head in frustration. 'But you *can* cope, because Frank is *always* with you. You have him under control right now and you don't even realise it. That's how strong you are.'

Ruby rubs her temples and groans. 'But...'

'No *buts*, Ruby.' I shoot her a stern stare as we turn onto her lane. 'Aldo and I had this same conversation just last night. We cannot let our anxiety control our lives any more than it already has.'

'You sound annoyed.' She whispers, twirling a strand of hair around her finger tensely.

'I *am* bloody annoyed!' My face flushes violently and I bang my hand on the steering wheel. 'I've had enough. Enough of anxiety, enough of fear and enough of people not going after their dreams. This is being handed to you on a plate. If you don't grab this with both hands, you will look back and regret it.'

I can hear the desperation as I speak, but there's little I can do to control it. I *am* desperate. I am desperate for Ruby to believe in herself. I start to prepare a motivational speech in my mind, but as we approach the farm, I decide to keep it to myself. Pushing someone too hard in one direction almost always results in them going the other way.

Forcing myself to smile, I wave at Yvette as we pull onto the driveway. Jabbing her pitchfork into a mound of hay, she tugs off her gloves and makes her way over to the car. Ruby curses under her breath and I pretend I haven't heard her.

'Hi!' I shield my eyes from the afternoon sun as Yvette leans into the window. 'I've just spent the last twenty minutes trying to talk Ruby into going on this work trip...'

'I wouldn't waste your time.' Yvette scoffs and motions for Ruby to get out of the car. 'She won't leave Cheshire, let alone leave the country!'

I stare back at her, a little stumped by her reaction. 'But this is an amazing opportunity for her. Travelling is all she has talked about for the past six months...'

'And in another six months she will be talking about something else.' Yvette laughs sarcastically and pulls open the passenger door. 'I appreciate your concern, but until she drops the anxiety stuff, she isn't going to do anything with her life.'

Ruby raises her eyebrows at me and slides out of her seat. I open my mouth to speak, but the truth is, I really don't know what to say. I'm completely lost for words. Ruby has mentioned her mum's dismissive attitude towards her anxiety a few times, but I never imagined she could be as flippant as this.

I raise my hand and wave to Ruby as she follows her mum into the barn. Half of me wants to get out of the car and chase after them. Yvette needs to know how detrimental her response to Ruby's mental health is, but it's not my place to tell her. I don't want to wade in on their personal relationship and potentially destroy the already weak bond they have.

Promising myself to speak to Ruby about it, I put the car into gear and do a three-point turn in the gravel. Resting my hand on the gear stick, I grab the steering wheel with my spare hand as I come face to face with The Shepard. Is Aidan in there right now? Has he gone back to Surrey? Creeping forwards, I bite my lip and hover over the indicator. I should go left. I should be heading back home. I'm not at work now. Whatever Aidan does in his spare time is none of my business.

Hitting the indicator, I press my foot on the accelerator before swiftly hitting the breaks. Something inside me is pulling me towards the bed and breakfast. I have to call in there. I need to know that he is alright.

Quickly turning the car around, I pull on the handbrake and run inside the building. The musky smell hangs thickly in the air as I look around the remote hallway. Should I just go upstairs? Spotting the elderly man, who I presume to be Leonard, I walk into the dining area.

'I'm looking for Aidan Wilder?' I say quietly, hoping that I've remembered his last name correctly. 'Is he here?'

Leonard takes a shabby book from the cabinet on his left and runs a finger along the handwritten list of names.

'Aidan Wilder.' He repeats, closing the book again. 'He's in Room Three. He came back a short while ago.'

'Is it okay to go up?' I ask, already turning to face the stairs.

Leonard nods and returns to polishing his tray of cutlery, leaving me free to go in search of Aidan.

My heart pounds in my chest as I make my way up the creaky staircase. The steps groan under my feet, just as they did the last time I was here. Coming to a stop in front of the room I know to be Aidan's, I raise my hand to knock, before dropping it down by my side. What am I doing? What the hell am I going to say to him? Doubt consumes me as my heart pounds in embarrassment. I have to put a stop to this. I have to stop being ruled by my emotions and overstepping the mark. I don't think Julia took it upon herself to go in search of Anxiety Anonymous attendees when they missed a meeting.

Having a change of heart, I slowly turn around, taking care to not make a sound as I reach for the railing. The moment my foot hits the first step the floorboard creaks noisily beneath me. Swearing under my breath, I grimace as I hear a door squeak open. Slowly looking up, my stomach drops as light floods into the lobby, revealing a confused Aidan staring directly at me...

Chapter 21

'Sadie?' He mutters in astonishment. 'What are you doing here?'

Suddenly feeling rather stupid, I try to think of something to say. Anything that doesn't make me sound like a crazed stalker. Temporarily losing the ability to speak, I eventually manage to regain the use of my tongue.

'I was worried about you.' I mumble, trying to stop my cheeks from flushing. 'I just wanted to make sure you were okay and now that I can see you are, I'll leave...'

Reaching for the banister, I decide to make a quick escape when Aidan's voice hits me.

'Wait!'

Stopping in my tracks, I look over my shoulder to see him holding the door to his room open. Knowing that I can't decline after boldly coming in here, I exhale slowly and hesitantly follow him into the room. The dated suite is exactly as I remember it, except this time, there's a half-packed suitcase on the bed.

'You're leaving?' I ask, my heart sinking as I point to the case.

Aidan looks between the case and me and back again. 'I am.' He says finally, an uncertain edge to his voice.

'Where are you going?' Noticing that his suitcase contains nothing more than a couple of pairs of jeans and a handful of t-shirts, I realise just how little he must have brought with him.

'That's the question I have been asking myself for the past two days.' Aidan sighs and perches on the foot of the bed. 'Where do I go from here?'

Taking a seat in the armchair opposite him, I fumble with the sleeve of my shirt and wait for him to elaborate.

'That day I spent with you made me feel more alive than I have in a very long time. You gave me the courage to believe that I *do* have a future. I watched your car drive away and immediately grabbed the suitcase. That glimmer of normality brought me back to life.' He pauses and runs his hands through his hair. 'I had this sudden surge of determination, but once I started throwing things into the case, I realised I didn't know where the hell I was going.'

Resting my elbows on my knees, I listen intently as Aidan lets out a groan.

'I tossed and turned all night, desperately trying to work out where I should go. I sold our house, so it's not like I have a home to go to. I haven't spoken to any of my friends in almost a year. My sister and I don't get along at the best of times...' He throws his arms in the air and laughs ironically. 'The funny thing is, my finances make the world my playground. I can go anywhere I want to.'

Aidan's eyes crinkle into a sad smile as he looks down at his bare ring finger.

'Where would you go.' I whisper. 'If you could click your fingers and be anywhere at all, even just for an hour. Where would you go?'

'I honestly don't know.' He replies, without a flicker of hesitation. 'Mel would know what to do. I would give anything to be able to talk to her just one more time.'

Aidan pushes himself up and stands by the window. Resting his hands on his hips, he spins around decidedly.

'That's where I would go. I would go and speak to Mel. We scattered her ashes in the forest where we used to walk. She loved it there.'

I stare at him in silence, unable to comprehend just how painful this must be for him.

'Why don't you go there? To the forest? It might bring you some clarity to be in a place where you feel close to her?'

He sighs heavily and shakes his head. 'I don't think I could do it. I haven't been back there since the day we scattered her ashes.'

I purse my lips and watch Aidan pace back and forth around the room. 'I think it would do you good. I really do believe this could be a positive move for you. Sometimes, the hardest thing you can imagine doing is exactly what you need. It might help to bring you closure...'

'Closure?' He repeats, a look of horror on his face. 'I don't want to get closure. The last thing on earth that I want to do is forget about Mel.'

'I am in no way suggesting that you have closure on your marriage, but you need closure on your grief in order to look to the future.' I slowly step towards him and place a tentative hand on his shoulder. 'It's clear for anyone to see that your grief is eating you up inside. It's tearing you apart and I am sure Mel wouldn't want that. Accepting your grief will enable you to move forward. You have said yourself that you want to go back there. Sometimes, our subconscious knows what's best for us, even if we don't believe it ourselves.'

Aidan turns to face me and folds his arms. 'I guess that makes sense, I just honestly don't think I could go back there.' His eyes burn into mine and an immense sadness washes over me. 'If I go, will you come with me?'

My stomach flips and I feel my jaw sag open.

'I'm sorry. I'm so sorry, Sadie.' He holds his head in his hands and looks away. 'I shouldn't be putting you in that position.'

Totally lost for words, I watch Aidan mentally beat himself up.

'I just feel so alone up here. I don't know a single other person to ask, but that's not your problem. You've been so nice to me and you didn't need to be. Please, forget that I said anything...'

'I'll go.' I whisper, before I know what I'm saying.

Aidan slowly turns around and stares at me in shock. 'You will?'

I nod back at him, already concerned at the prospect of explaining this one to Aldo.

'You would really do that for me?' Aidan gushes, unable to hide how touched he is by my offer. 'Are you sure?'

'Yes.' My skin prickles as I realise what I've just agreed to, making me feel incredibly uneasy. 'When do you want to go?'

'You tell me. I can make myself available whenever you are'.

I cover my eyes with my hands as I rack my brains for my schedule. 'I'm not working this Saturday. Do you think we could get there and back in a day?'

'That's a lot of driving, but it's definitely doable...'

As Aidan reels off the route, I try to calm my racing heart. It's one day. Just a single day. What could possibly go wrong?

'I'll sort the transport.' Aidan announces, grabbing his suitcase and placing it on the floor. 'Leave everything to me and I'll pick you up on Saturday morning. How about ten? Does that work for you?'

I look back at him in bewilderment. This is the most animated I have ever seen him. As I try to decode his behaviour, I suddenly become annoyed with myself. Who am I to say what is the normal way to behave after losing your spouse? *Is* there a normal way to behave after losing your spouse?

'Saturday works for me.' I smile thinly, very aware that I have just three days to prepare myself.

Aidan beams brightly, colour rushing back to his drained face. 'Thank you so much for this, Sadie. I won't ever forget it.'

I nod in response as the sun starts to set, causing the room to fall into shadow. Taking this as my cue to leave, I grab my handbag and clear my throat.

'I should be going...'

'Of course!' Dashing over to the door, Aidan pulls it open and holds out his hand.

I look at it cautiously for a few seconds, before giving in and reluctantly accepting it. Shaking his hand feels weird, but a hug would be highly inappropriate.

'So, will we be seeing you at the meeting on Friday?' I ask, as I head for the stairs.

His smile momentarily falters and he shrugs his shoulders. 'I don't know. Maybe.'

'Maybe.' I repeat, happy that *maybe* is better than *no*...

Chapter 22

Peering through the glass, I watch Ruby's face light up as she chats to an elderly couple from behind her desk. Happiness shines out of her as she points at pictures of clear waters in a glossy brochure. The couple nod along as she flips through the pages, chatting animatedly about the array of beautiful images. Ruby was made for this job. It would be a crime for her to miss the Caribbean trip.

Suddenly looking up from her keyboard, she gives me a quick wave and wraps up the conversation. As I wait for her to gather her things, I take a moment to study the many adverts in the window display. I can't remember the last time I felt soft sand between my toes. Oh, how tempting it is to hand over the plastic and book yourself on a one-way ticket to paradise. Reminding myself I shall soon be taking a trip of my own, I bite my lip anxiously and try to push it to the back of my mind.

Today, Ruby and I are going to distress some furniture I picked up at the local charity shop, over an elderflower cocktail, or two. Although, I must confess to having an ulterior motive and that is to ensure Ruby agrees to go on the Caribbean trip. I know I can't physically force her into it, but if I don't at least try, I will kick myself later. I've got a sneaky feeling that her refusal to go for this has more to do with her mother than anything else.

'Hey!' Ruby pushes her way out onto the busy street, effectively stopping my train of thought. 'How are you?'

'I'm good.' I link my arm through hers as we automatically head towards Blossom View.

'We're walking?' She asks, suddenly aware that we've passed the car park.

I nod in response and smile. The absence of my car is another part of my plan to coax Ruby. 'With the sun shining so brightly, it would almost be a crime to take the car.'

'That's true.' She shields her eyes from the strong rays and stares up at the blue sky overhead. 'Don't you just love days like this?'

'I do.' I pause and give her a sideways glance. 'Just think, you could have eight whole weeks of sunshine to look forward to! Antigua, Aruba, Barbados...'

She rolls her eyes and yawns loudly. 'I've told myself that ten times already today...'

'Well, are you going to listen to yourself?' I ask, giving her a playful nudge. 'Or do you need to say it one more time?'

'Why don't *you* go, if you're so taken with the idea?' She grumbles, plucking her sunglasses from her vintage handbag.

'Maybe one day I will, but now isn't my time. It's yours.' I reply, as we simultaneously duck beneath a flowering tree. 'Please don't let Frank stop you from doing this.'

'To be honest, it's no longer about Frank.' Ruby smiles sadly as we walk past the school. 'It's about my mum.'

Anger bubbles in the pit of my stomach as my suspicions are confirmed. I knew this would happen. If you are continually told that you will fail, you start to believe it.

'I don't want to sound disrespectful towards your mother, Ruby, but please, don't listen to a word she says.'

'Usually, I don't, but because I was already sceptical of the trip, her doubts have sealed the deal for me.'

Refusing to allow Yvette victory, I silently consider my next move. 'Do you *want* to go? If you don't, just say the word and I promise I will drop it.'

'You know I want to go!' Ruby moans, folding her arms in frustration. 'Who wouldn't?'

'Then do it for me!' A sudden surge of adrenaline rushes through my veins and I take her by the shoulders. 'Do it for all the people at Anxiety Anonymous. If you can't do it for yourself, then do it for them.'

A couple of schoolgirls walk past and shoot us a funny look. I must admit that we probably do look rather strange. I am literally begging Ruby in the middle of the street, not caring in the slightest that people are staring.

'Fine!' She eventually hisses, knocking my hands from her shoulders. 'Now will you please drop this?'

Nodding in response, I let out an ecstatic squeal and throw my arms around her neck. 'You're making the right decision! This will be a huge turning point for you...'

Ruby cuts me off abruptly by holding up her hands. 'You said you would drop it!'

Silently screaming with joy, I pretend to zip my mouth shut as we continue on our walk. Glancing at her out of the corner of my eye, I inwardly high-five myself as I notice a huge smile spreading across her face. She will thank me for this one day. This will be a monumental milestone in her life, it's just going to take a little while for her to realise it...

* * *

It turns out that it didn't take long at all for Ruby to realise how exciting this Caribbean trip is going to be, as just two hours and an elderflower cocktail later, she's animatedly planning her suitcase with me.

'Is the weather hot all year round in the Caribbean?' She asks, sitting cross-legged in the garden and dipping her cloth into the tin of varnish.

'It certainly is.' I grin back at her and shoo Mateo away from the sticky polish. 'You do get rainy seasons, but it will never be terribly cold.'

'So, no UGG boots?' She leans across the cabinet and tackles a bare patch of wood beneath the drawers.

'Definitely not!' I let out a giggle and take a step back to get a better view of the cabinet. 'Aldo is going to be *so* jealous. With Edward sunning himself in California he is just itching for a sunshine break. I can't wait to tell him.'

'I'm dreading telling my mum.' Abandoning her cloth, Ruby stretches out on the grass, causing Mateo to immediately bound over to her. 'She didn't believe for a second that I would be brave enough to go.'

'Why don't you just call her?' I ask, joining her on the lawn. 'Some things are easier to say over the phone.'

Ruby sighs and looks up at the sky reflectively. 'I should really wait until I have spoken to my manager at Escapism. Besides, *nothing* is easy to say to my mum when she doesn't want to hear it.'

I nod along, completely understanding her dilemma. 'My mum is exactly the same. You've seen how difficult she can be.'

'I have, but it's always worse when it's your own mother. I just wish she would talk to me like an adult, you know? She still dismisses my thoughts and feelings as though I'm a child, but you know what? Mum doesn't always know best.'

I sit quietly for a moment, letting her words sink in and thinking back to all the times where my own mother has been wrong. 'That's true, but I'm sure Yvette would be devastated if you told her how she makes you feel.'

'Would yours?' She fires back doubtfully, not missing a beat.

My mind flits to the time our paths last crossed and I recall her face as I told her I loved her. 'Probably not, but you should speak to her.'

'About the trip?'

'About everything. You only get one mother...'

For a while, we both lay there in complete silence, happily watching the clouds float past above our heads. Feeling myself start to relax, I trace the outline of each ball of fluff that passes, trying to figure out what they represent. Spotting one that resembles a fuzzy dog, my smile freezes as I'm mentally transported back to the forest. As much as I don't want to believe it, if it wasn't for that elderly man and his beloved pet, I dread to think what would have happened.

Not wanting to ruin a beautiful afternoon by obsessing over what could have been, I roll onto my side and face Ruby. Blissfully pointing out the different shapes, she looks so carefree and content. If Ruby can conquer her anxiety and fly to the Caribbean for two months, I'm pretty sure I can move on from my brief relapse.

With each dose of Ann, I become stronger and better equipped to control her. I will not live in fear of my anxiety. I may crumble, I may fall down and feel unable to carry on, but no matter what, I *will* get back up again...

Chapter 23

'It looks great in here!' I gush, wandering around Aldo's living room with wide eyes. 'I see Edward finally let you paint over the feature wall?'

'Edward isn't here, so Edward doesn't have a say.' Aldo throws his hair over his shoulder and perches on the windowsill.

I raise my eyebrows and smile to myself, picturing Edward's face when he finds out his beloved hand-drawn Banyan tree is no more.

'So, to what do I owe this honour?' Aldo asks, checking out his nail varnish. 'You haven't been over here in weeks. What's going on?'

'Nothing!' I giggle nervously and shake my head. 'Can't a girl visit her best friend anymore?'

Aldo squints at me suspiciously and frowns. 'Spit it out. I've got a blow dry in an hour.'

I exhale loudly and roll my eyes, suddenly regretting my decision to drop by. 'I'm going to Surrey tomorrow.'

'Surrey?' Aldo repeats in confusion. 'What for?'

Biting my lip, I clear my throat and try to sound nonchalant. 'Aidan asked me...'

'Who?' Aldo cuts me off mid-sentence. 'Who the hell is Aidan?'

'The guy from Anxiety Anonymous.' Blood rushes to my face as he stares back at me. 'You've met him. He came to Blossom View to assess the building work.'

Aldo holds up his hand to silence me. '*That* guy? What does he have to do with anything?'

Already knowing how this conversation is going to go, I blurt it out as quickly as I can. 'I've encouraged him to visit the place where he scattered his late wife's ashes and he's asked me to join him.'

Aldo glares at me with a look I can't decipher. 'What the hell are you talking about?'

'Please don't overreact.'

'Overreact?' Aldo repeats coolly, rapping his fingers on the windowsill. 'What do you even know about this guy?'

'I know that he needs help...'

'Isn't that the truth.'

Not wanting an argument, I twirl a piece of hair around my fingers and look away.

'Shirley, just try and see this from my point of view. This guy has rocked up to a support group, spun you a sob story and now he's taking you hundreds of miles away. He couldn't be more suspect if he tried.'

'That's not fair. Aidan's struggling right now, just like I was a few months back, only he doesn't have a fabulous best friend to help him through it.'

Tucking my hair behind my ears, I take a step towards him. 'It's just one day. I will be there and back before you know it. Just think, if I thought I was doing something wrong, I would have kept this to myself. I'm telling you because it's no big deal.'

Aldo shakes his head and rests his hands on his hips. 'I've got a really bad feeling about this.'

'It will be *fine*.' I attempt a little laugh, but cut it short when he doesn't join in. 'I just need you to trust me, can you do that?'

He scowls like a petulant child and collapses onto the couch in a heap. 'Fine, but like I said, I've got a really bad feeling about it.'

Taking this as an end to the conversation, I breathe a sigh of relief and sit down next to him. 'Did Ruby tell you she's going on the Caribbean trip?'

'You're kidding?' Aldo groans, looking genuinely disappointed. 'With Edward in America, Ruby globetrotting the Caribbean and you in Surrey, what am *I* going to do?'

'You can hang out with Mateo for the day.' I tease, letting out a snigger as he shoots me a deathly glare.

'On a better note, I spoke with Pierce last night.' He grumbles, flicking through the television stations.

'That's great.' My stomach flips as I remember I actually agreed to date this guy. 'I'm pretty busy these next few weeks, but I'm sure we will be able to sort something out...'

'You're going for dinner at Il Migliore with him next Friday.'

'Next Friday?' I repeat, suddenly feeling incredibly sick.

'You heard me. He's taking you to your favourite restaurant, so you've got absolutely nothing to complain about.' He flashes me a stern stare and shoves a cushion behind his head. 'You're going to go, you're going to enjoy it and you're going to return telling me that I found you the most perfect man on the planet.'

I smile back at him, trying to hide my anxiety over the impending meeting behind a grin. The idea of a blind date petrifies me and Aldo knows that. Being matched with a mystery man isn't how I pictured myself getting back into the dating game, but life doesn't always go according to plan. Sometimes, you just need to breathe, trust, let go of your reservations and simply see what happens...

Chapter 24

Standing on the doorstep, I peek at my watch for what feels like the millionth time. Aidan should have been here ten minutes ago, but so far, there's no sign of him. Half of me is secretly hoping he's had a last-minute change of heart and decided to go to Surrey alone.

After a restless night's sleep, I have contemplated my decision to join him on this trip all morning. Should I really be taking myself so far out of my comfort zone? Is Aldo right? Is this a terrible idea? So many doubts have been running through my mind, but the counsellor in me is ignoring them.

Before I have the chance to overthink it, I spot a vintage Porsche 911 slowly creeping along the lane. Squinting through the windscreen, I'm shocked to discover Aidan is in the driver's seat. The classic car comes to a steady stop in front of Blossom View and I slowly make my way down the gravel path.

'I'm so sorry I'm late.' He smiles apologetically and leans over to open the passenger door. 'I had a little car trouble.'

'Whose car is this?' I ask, sliding into my seat and admiring the retro features of the interior.

'It's Leonard's. He kindly let me borrow it for the day.' Aidan fiddles with the dashboard until the radio picks up a signal. 'It did take us a little while to get the battery going, but it's purring like a kitten now.'

I smile in response as we pull away from the pavement and immediately fall into silence. Suddenly aware that we have a very long drive ahead of us, I feel my stomach churn once more. We have been in the car together for less than five minutes and I already can't think of anything to say. Fidgeting with my watch, I look out of the window and try to come up with something to fill the deafening silence.

'Have you been to Surrey before?' Aidan asks, resting his elbow on the armrest.

I turn to face him, so thankful to have something to talk about. 'I have not. Aldo and I have taken many trips to London. There was a point where we were there every weekend, but never Surrey.'

'I love London. It's the greatest city in the world.' Aidan smiles as we head towards the motorway. 'Is London as far south as you have got?'

'I used to spend a lot of time in Brighton.' I mumble, an awful feeling running through me as I recall my time on the coast of England.

'Brighton!' Aidan repeats happily. 'Another of my favourite places. The Lanes were Mel's escape from reality. The quaint shops, the quirky boutiques and the unique charm of the place consumed us.'

I smile in response, knowing all too well how beautiful The Lanes are. Unfortunately, my memories of them are tainted with the heartache that occurred there.

'It seems to be shaping up to be a nice day after all.' I muse, taking a stab at changing the subject. 'The weather forecast predicted heavy rain, but there isn't a cloud in the sky.'

'It will certainly make the travelling easier.' Aidan puts up the window to block out the sound of the wind. 'I calculated it online and the journey should take around four hours, more or less.'

My skin prickles as I realise just how long this road trip is going to take.

'Don't worry, I'll have you back before the sun goes down.' Aidan teases. 'I can't thank you enough for doing this. If you weren't with me, there's no way I would ever have come back. I can't imagine many other people would do what you're doing.'

I smile back at him, my face turning red at his compliments.

'Did you get your damp sorted?' He asks, clearly sensing my embarrassment as we turn onto the motorway. 'If you leave it much longer it will spread to other parts of your home and slowly rot them. Ignoring the problem is just intensifying the problem. The longer you leave it, the worse it will become.'

I listen to his words, remarking at how they could also be used to describe anxiety. 'I'll sort it soon.'

'Make sure you do. Once it's in there, it will eat away at parts you didn't even know existed.'

'Don't worry.' I reply, ignoring the queasiness in my stomach. 'I know all too well how that can happen...'

Chapter 25

We must have been driving for around two hours when I get the uncontrollable urge to stretch my legs. Repeatedly rotating my ankles has finally proven useless and if I don't get out soon, I might just cease up completely.

'Would it be possible to have a toilet stop soon?' I ask, fidgeting uncomfortably in my seat.

'No problem. We need to stop for petrol shortly, anyway.' Aidan nods and points at the sat nav. 'Can you hold out for another fifteen minutes?'

Glancing at the screen, I realise that I don't really have a choice as the next service station is miles away. Crossing my legs in a poor attempt at getting comfortable, I tap my fingers in time to the music as we tear down the motorway. Humming along to the music, I jolt forward as the car suddenly bumps and a loud thudding sound overtakes the radio.

'What was that?' I gasp, trying not to be alarmed as Aidan frowns and leans over the steering wheel.

The car jerks for a second time before the rumbling noise intensifies.

'Sh...' Aidan curses under his breath and grips the steering wheel tightly. 'I think we have a tyre out.'

'A tyre out?' I repeat, sticking my head out of the window to check if he's right.

Putting his hazard lights on, Aidan swiftly manoeuvres the car onto the hard shoulder. Hoping it's something that can be easily fixed, I unclip my seatbelt and push open the passenger door. A stream of cars fire past as Aidan instructs me to stay on the embankment. Trying to stop my hair from blowing into my lipstick, I shield my eyes from the sun as he crouches down next to the front left wheel.

'We've got a puncture.' He confirms, pulling a large nail out of the very flat tyre.

'So, what do we do?' I reply, fumbling with the zip of my jacket to fasten it. 'How do we fix it?'

Aidan rubs his face and groans. 'Unless Leonard has a spare, we're going to have to phone for roadside assistance.'

I cross my fingers as he opens the boot and shakes his head. 'Roadside assistance it is.'

He smiles apologetically and digs his phone out of his pocket. 'I'm sorry about this. I'll give them a call and we should be back on the road in no time at all.'

'It's no problem. These things happen.' I flash him the thumbs up sign and walk a short distance up the embankment, giving him some space to make the call.

Taking a seat on the dry grass, I rest my elbows on my knees and watch the flurry of cars race past. Despite the wind, the sun is still shining brightly and I couldn't be more thankful. This could have been a whole lot worse if the weather would have taken a turn for the worse. Fishing my sunglasses out of my handbag, I take a moment to check my phone. I contemplate calling Aldo, but decide against it when Aidan starts to walk towards me.

'Well?' I ask, searching his face for clues as to the outcome. 'What did they say?'

Dropping onto the ground, he tosses his handset next to him and copies my position. 'They should have someone here within the hour. Hopefully, it won't be too long.'

I take a quick look around and wipe my hands on my jeans. 'There doesn't seem to be anything nearby. Should we wait up here or do you want to sit in the car until they get here?'

'No!' He yells, taking me aback by the fury in his voice. 'You shouldn't ever sit on the hard shoulder!'

I stare at him in shock, completely stunned by his reaction. 'Okay...' I mumble, suddenly feeling a little uncomfortable. 'Then we will just wait here.'

'If you ever have car trouble on a motorway, the first thing you do is get out of the damn vehicle and get to a safe place!'

My skin prickles at his sharp words and I look down at the ground in embarrassment. Suddenly remembering his comments about Mel being in a road accident, I decide to come straight out with it.

'What happened to Mel, Aidan?' I whisper, my voice barely audible over the sound of the traffic.

For a short while, he doesn't say a word. He just sits there, staring at the motorway in an eerie silence. His face is blank and expressionless as my heart races in my chest.

'We were in Thailand. After so many years of talking about travelling, we were finally living our dream.'

I exhale slowly, hardly daring to breathe as he finally speaks.

'Mel was so happy. The joy would just shine out of her like a rainbow. From the moment she opened her eyes, she would be beaming brightly. I can still see that smile as though she's standing right in front of me. The way her eyes would crinkle, the childlike sound of her laugh and the dimple in her left cheek. She was just... *perfect*.'

Plucking a daisy from the glass, he rhythmically tears off the petals.

'We had been there for twelve weeks when it happened. It was a Friday and we were due to fly home the following week. The plan was to stay there for six months, but at the halfway mark, Mel told me she had finally washed the wanderlust out of her hair. As we watched the sunrise on the beach, she spontaneously announced that she wanted to start a family. She was ready for home and to be truthful, so was I. Hearing her say she wanted a baby made me the happiest man on the planet. It was as though one adventure was coming to an end and another was just beginning. Right there, at that very moment, my life felt complete. I had everything I could ever have wanted.'

A lump forms in my throat and I try desperately to swallow it.

'When we told everyone we were leaving, they threw us the mother of all parties. We danced until the sun came up with all of the friends we had made on our journey. It was the perfect end to the perfect adventure. Or at least, it *would* have been the perfect end...'

Aidan's voice starts to wobble and I rest a reassuring hand on his arm.

'Mel had befriended an elderly lady in the next village. She was too sick to attend the party, so Mel woke up at dawn to pay her one last visit and say her goodbyes. She asked me to go with her, but I was just so tired from the party. I'll never forgive myself for letting her go alone.'

He pauses for breath and tosses the final daisy petal into the grass.

'She kissed me goodbye and with that, she was gone. That was the last time I ever saw her. The next thing I remember, I was being woken by our neighbour. He was frantic. I couldn't understand a word he was saying, but I knew something horrible had happened. The panic in his eyes is something I will never forget.'

The roaring from the motorway fills the air, but all I can hear is Aidan's sorrowful voice.

'Mel never made it to her friend's house. There was a tree in the road, she swerved and lost control of the car. She died instantly...'

My blood runs cold as the magnitude of what he is saying hits me. This is a million times worse than I imagined. Mel's life was cut short by a horrific accident before it had properly begun. They had so much to look forward to, they had so much life to live.

'Aidan, I'm so, *so* sorry.'

Refusing to make eye contact, Aidan blinks repeatedly as his eyes gloss over.

'It was widely covered by the press. They lapped it up. The media were like vultures. For weeks, I had cameras in my face asking me how I felt, but I didn't feel anything. Half of the time, I didn't even know what was happening. I was passed from pillar to post. There was so much paperwork. So much sitting around in offices, when all I wanted to do was breakdown and cry. I remember being in a room, with a dozen suited men who were speaking a language I couldn't understand. I wanted to scream. I couldn't comprehend how they could be acting so normal when my wife, my Mel, had just died.'

I clasp my hands over my mouth as tears slip down my cheeks.

'The idea of returning without her was too much, so I stayed until they released her body. The whole journey home, I stared at the stranger beside me in shock. I was numb. I was numb for months. People tried to gather around me. My family and my friends were desperate to help, but I just wanted to be alone. I shut everyone out. The funeral was the first time I allowed them to see me. They were horrified by my appearance and I can understand why. I wasn't eating properly. I wasn't sleeping. I was just existing in those four walls. Some days, I wouldn't even know if I was dead or alive.'

He pauses and runs his thumb over his bare ring finger.

'After the funeral, I hit rock bottom. I spent months trying to figure out a way to get my life back, but every avenue seemed pointless. I didn't want a life without Mel. I considered calling it a day, pressing *game over* and tapping out, but something stopped me every time. Almost six months passed without her and I still hadn't left the house for anything more than food. I just didn't have the energy or the patience to do anything anymore. That's when I went back to Thailand. I thought that maybe, just maybe, I would feel closer to her there. The second we touched down on Thai soil, I knew I had made a mistake. The memories of her were everywhere and the sorrowful looks started all over again.'

Aidan rubs his face wearily and I discreetly wipe away my tears.

'I spent less than a week there before returning to England. Walking into the empty house that used to hold so much laughter and happiness killed me. That house was the place where we were going to live out our future. I couldn't stay there. Waking up in the bed where we once slept was like losing her over and over again. Making the decision to sell was tough. Half of me felt like I was giving away the last piece of her. The four months it took to sell seemed to take forever. I questioned myself so much during that time. Was I doing the right thing or was I running away from what was now my reality?'

An ambulance fires down the motorway, causing him to pause for a moment before picking up where he left off.

'The day the sale went through, I had all of my belongings put into storage. If it didn't fit in my backpack or the suitcase, it wasn't coming with me. My family asked me where I was going, but I didn't know myself. I got a taxi to the train station and jumped on the first one that came in. I changed in a few locations, literally plucking trains at random. By nightfall, I found myself in Mobberley. Having no clue where I was, I just walked out of the station and kept on going. I turned onto a secluded lane and walked through nothingness for what felt like an eternity.'

Completely mesmerised by his story, I suddenly realise I have been holding my breath and force myself to inhale.

'Just as I was going to give up and turn back, I saw The Shepard. It was like a sign, a sign from Mel.

Showing me the way and guiding me to safety. I was there for two weeks before I ventured out. I had completely lost track of the time. Even the days, weeks and months had blurred into one. When I realised what the date was, I just had to get out of there. A whole year had passed me by and I still wasn't any closer to dealing with what happened. When I left the B&B, I didn't know where I was going, but an hour of walking led me to Wilmslow. That's when I saw the sign for your meeting and something inside me drew me to the door. Realising it was the anniversary of Mel's death nearly broke me, but stumbling into that building saved me from doing something very stupid.'

For the first time, Aidan brings his eyes up to meet mine and I feel my heart ache with sorrow.

'So, there you have it. You wanted to understand how I found myself at your support group, now you know…'

Chapter 26

Completely lost for words, I open and close my mouth repeatedly, desperately searching for the correct thing to say. Before I can breathe a word, Aidan pushes himself to his feet and walks away. Salty tears splash into my lap and I bat them away furiously. Everyone who walks through the door at Anxiety Anonymous has a story regarding how they got there, but Aidan's tops the lot. My heart is breaking for him. I can't even begin to imagine what he has been through. A part of me wonders how he's still standing. How do you find the strength to pick yourself up after something so terribly horrific?

I turn to look at him and wipe my cheeks with my sleeve. Standing at the top of the embankment, with his hands on his hips as the cars race by below him, Aidan lets the tears spill down his cheeks. How can life be so cruel, so fragile and so susceptible to destruction? All the ideas I conjured up about Aidan's past don't touch the surface to the reality of his life. I feel so helpless, so useless and so out of my depth. Just how do you help someone who has been through what Aidan has?

As I stare at him, wondering what on earth I can do to fix the gaping hole in his life, a huge yellow van pulls up next to the Porsche. Immediately snapping back to attention, Aidan dries his eyes. Waving to the recovery men, I hastily compose myself as Aidan heads down to the hard shoulder.

'It's the front left.' He explains casually, shoving his hands into his pockets as the guys get to work on replacing the damaged wheel.

Giving them some space, I leave them to expertly deal with the mishap. Aidan makes small talk, completely detached from the man who just poured his heart out on the embankment. I've seen glimpses of that man before, but it's clear that it took a whole lot of courage for him to have that conversation. I am so shocked and saddened by what he's told me that I genuinely don't know what to do with myself. Where do we go from here?

'Sadie?' Aidan's voice bursts my thought bubble and I look up to see the recovery men handing him a slip of paper. 'We're ready to go.'

Forcing a small smile, I slowly make my way over to him and slide into the passenger seat. Aidan starts the engine and we continue our journey in an emotional silence. As we gather up speed to join the motorway, I steal a glance at him.

'I've never told anyone that before...' He murmurs, keeping his eyes fixed on the road ahead. 'I've actually never mentioned Mel's name to anyone before now.'

I look down into my lap and run my thumb over my finger tattoo. 'Well, I am incredibly touched that you confided in me and I am so terribly sorry for your loss...'

'Please, I don't want your sympathy.' Aidan's brow furrows and he shakes his head. 'I can't bear it.'

I nod along, choosing my words carefully. 'How do you feel now that you have finally spoken about it?'

Aidan rubs his forehead and shrugs his shoulders sadly. 'Raw, devastated, but weirdly, a little lighter. I can't really explain it. It's almost as though I can breathe a little deeper.'

'Lighter is good.' I say encouragingly, turning down the radio so that I can hear him more clearly. 'I really think you would benefit from some in-depth counselling. More advanced than I can offer...'

'No. I've tried that. All those doctors and people in white coats look at me in a way that makes me want to run a million miles away. You don't look at me like that.'

I raise my eyebrows, completely understanding the fear of counselling and everything that comes with it. 'I remember feeling like that. The thought of talking to someone was horrific, but there came a point where I was willing to try anything in the hope it would make me feel like my normal self again.'

'That's where we're different. I'll *never* feel like my normal self again. Part of me died with Mel and I will never get it back.'

We approach a congested junction and I purse my lips while Aidan works his way through the patch of traffic.

'What led *you* to Anxiety Anonymous?' He asks, as the motorway finally clears. 'I've told you my story. What's yours?'

My heart drops as I think back to my own experience with anxiety. 'It was a series of things, really. I went through a breakup, I lost my job and I discovered who my biological father was. I didn't realise it at the time, but one blow after the next sent me into an anxiety-fuelled depression. I crumbled. I watched the person I was slowly fade away and I was powerless to stop it. The support group saved me from my anxiety and more importantly, it saved me from myself.'

I feel the atmosphere change and pretend I haven't noticed.

'I'm so sorry, Sadie.'

He offers me a sympathetic smile and I shake it off. 'Now it's my turn to refuse the sympathy.'

Aidan's lip curls into a tiny smile as he changes lane. 'Do you ever worry it will come back?'

An uncomfortable sensation washes over me as I think back to the day in the forest and nod. 'At first, I didn't think it would. For six months, I didn't have anything. Not so much as a glimpse of the cloud that once hung over me, but lately there have been a couple of occasions where that familiar dread and nauseating fear has crept back.'

'Do you have any idea why?' Aidan asks, as we finally turn off the motorway.

'I don't, but this time I'm able to stop the panic attack in its tracks. I can bring it back to a rational level before it gets out of control.' Adjusting my seatbelt, I pull a bobble from my wrist and twist my hair into a bun.

'It must be a great feeling to know you are in control of something that once knocked you down. The tables have turned. You're in charge now.' Aidan replies, flicking through the radio stations as the song we're listening to comes to an end.

'To be honest, I was just devastated that I felt that way again.' I confess. 'Even though it was just for a few minutes, in that moment, I was right back there. All of the emotions came flooding back and it was as though the last six months hadn't happened. I felt just as weak as I did back then.'

The car takes a sharp left and I look up to discover we're on an open road. With lush green trees lining the pavement and rolling countryside ahead, it feels strangely familiar. It's so much like home. If I didn't know any better, I would think I was back in Cheshire.

'But you weren't as weak. You kicked it to the kerb before it even got off the ground. That's amazing. You should be proud of yourself.' Aidan exclaims, bringing my focus back to the conversation.

'Ditto.' My cheeks flush and I give him a sideways smile. 'From what you've told me, you have come a very long way and I don't just mean geographically. We all cope with grief in different ways. Don't measure how you're dealing with this by anyone else's standards.'

'I must admit, I am guilty of that. I read so much online about the grief process and beat myself up because I wasn't following the same pattern. Knowing that I wasn't handling this normally made me completely lose it and I took my frustration out on everything around me. I would abuse my body with copious amounts of alcohol. I would punch walls in a poor bid at freeing myself from the pent-up anger inside me...'

I look down at his grazed knuckles and frown.

'Nothing worked. Nothing provided me with the release I craved. Not only was I completely broken, I was *useless* at being broken. I felt like I was letting Mel down. I couldn't even grieve correctly without her.'

'I'm sure Mel wouldn't want you to feel like that. She will be looking down on you with such incredible pride.' I try to reassure him by giving his forearm a friendly pat.

'I don't know about that. Mel was notorious for not pulling any punches. If she was here now, she would tell me to pour myself a stiff drink and pull myself together.' Aidan glances up at the sky and manages a tiny smile. 'I went through a stage of wishing it was me that had died. Mel would have handled this so much better than I have.'

'Just repeat that first part again...'

Aidan lets out a little laugh and indicates left. 'You're right. You're totally right. Mel would have loved you.'

My skin tingles and I smile in response as we pull onto a gravel entrance. Spotting a brown sign for Shingle Forest, I flip up the sun visor for a better view.

'Is this the place?' I ask, straining my neck for a better view of the abundant woodland ahead. 'It's beautiful.'

He nods and brings the car to a stop in an empty parking space. As he excuses himself to get a ticket, I push open the door and groan at the relief of finally being able to stretch out my legs. Taking in my surroundings, I lean against an old tree and have a quick scan around. The gravel car park leads to a wooden fence, which is conveniently located next to a signpost dictating the different parts of the woodland. The sound of children's laughter echoes through the trees in the distance, creating a beautiful soundtrack to the naturistic scene.

Stepping back, I shield my eyes from the sun and look up at the sky, marvelling at the height of the trees. Hearing footsteps behind me, I spin around to see Aidan placing a white slip in the windscreen. Waiting for him to lock the car, I study his face as he slams the door and takes a deep breath.

'Are you sure you want to do this?' I ask gently, very aware of the petrified look on his face. 'There's no pressure. We can get straight back in the car and head up to Cheshire. You just say the word and we'll leave.'

We hold eye contact for a few seconds, before Aidan shakes his head. 'No. I need to do this. Come on, it's this way...'

THE BIRD WHO DARES TO FALL,

IS THE BIRD WHO LEARNS TO FLY...

Chapter 27

Dry branches crunch beneath our feet as we trudge through the flurry of trees. The sun has unfortunately clouded over, but the air is still warm and humid. We have been walking for around twenty minutes, although the deathly silence makes it seem ten times longer. Despite not coming here since he scattered Mel's ashes, Aidan clearly knows exactly where he is going. Marching on ahead with a brisk determination, he hasn't hesitated once.

We come to a set of moss-covered steps, which are buried deep into the ground and I pause for breath as Aidan swiftly bounds to the bottom. Carefully putting one foot in front of the other, I slowly make my way down the slippery hill. Wiping my muddy hands on my jeans, I let out a gasp as I realise the steps have led us to a stunning stream. The water glistens as it rushes over the many pebbles and stones that are scattered through the babbling brook.

Too busy staring at the stunning scene in front of me, I don't realise that Aidan has stopped in his tracks. He doesn't need to breathe a word to let me know that this is the spot. I walk over to a rustic bench, which has been carved out of the trunk of a tree and silently perch on the edge. This is a monumental moment for Aidan and I don't want to influence it in any way. Standing perfectly still, he tips back his head and exhales deeply. His face is taught with emotion as he finally opens his eyes and stares at the stream intently.

I try to visualise what he is feeling right now. This is it. The is the final resting place of his beloved wife. This is the exact spot where he said his final goodbyes. My bottom lip starts to tremble and I blink back the tears as Aidan walks towards the stream and places both hands on the trunk of a huge tree. As though sensing the gravity of the moment, the birds stop chirping and the scene falls into an eerie silence. I watch the trees rustle all around him, shielding him from the wind whilst he tries to connect with Mel. I hope beyond hope that this is helping him. That this is giving him the closure he needs to accept what happened and finally start moving on with his life.

Acceptance seems to be the hardest thing with grief. No one wants to accept such a tragedy, but until they do, it is impossible to move on. No matter how many tears that fall, no matter how many times we pray for it not to be true, nothing will change the past. Nothing will turn back the clock and nothing will bring them back. Moving on doesn't mean forgetting what happened or leaving the memories behind, it simply means that you won't allow it to destroy your future as well as your past.

Suddenly turning around, Aidan slowly walks over to the bench. Taking a deep breath, he sits down next to me and rests his elbows on knees.

'It was right there in front of the stream.' He murmurs, emotion ringing through his strained voice. 'This was her favourite spot. After hours of hiking through the forest, we would finish off our time here with a picnic on this very bench.'

A strange sensation hits me as I picture Mel sat in this very spot, laughing with Aidan as they ate sandwiches and drank from flasks. I almost feel guilty for being here, for sitting in her place and for intruding on what was once hers.

'How do you feel?' I ask, pulling my jacket tightly around my body as a cold wind blows past us.

'I feel... I feel like I can finally let her go.' There's a long pause and when he finally looks at me, I realise he has tears in his eyes once more. 'Her memory shouldn't be tainted with my moping. She deserves to be remembered as the beautiful, joyful, zesty woman that she was. She breathed life into every room that she walked into. Her laugh was contagious and her heart was always full. When the rest of the world wanted to give up, she would push for one more try and that's what I have to do.'

Not daring to open my mouth in case I erupt into floods of tears, I nod back at him and desperately try to stop the tears from falling.

'It's been a year...' Aidan continues. 'A whole year. Three hundred and sixty-five painful days. This can't go on any longer. *I* can't go on any longer. It's chewing me up inside. I have to draw a line, carry on and take Mel with me. I don't have to grieve for her forever, I can see that now. I can have a life, I can have a future and keep Mel in here.' He taps his heart and lets his head drop slightly.

'I'm sure Mel would be incredibly proud of you right now...' I manage, wiping my face with the sleeve of my jacket. '*I'm* incredibly proud of you.'

Aidan wipes his own eyes and looks up at the sky once more, as tiny droplets of rain land on the tip of his nose. The drizzle slowly picks up pace, but neither of us move. We just sit there, allowing the rain to wash over us, not caring in the slightest that our clothes are rapidly becoming saturated. A flash of light shoots across the sky above us, shortly followed by a thunderous bang.

'We should be going.' Aidan clears his throat and stands to his feet, shielding his face from the heavy downpour.

'Are you sure you're ready to say goodbye?' I ask, squinting to see through the sheets of heavy rain. 'It's only a bit of water, we don't have to go yet if you're not ready.'

He takes one final look at the stream, before kissing his fingers and holding his hand up to the sky. 'I'm ready.'

Tugging up his hood, he starts to run in the direction of the car and motions for me to follow him. With a last glance over my shoulder, I brace myself against the harsh conditions and track Aidan's footsteps through the muddy paths. Despite picking up the pace, it still takes us a good ten minutes to return to the safety of the car.

Collapsing into the passenger seat, I look down at my soaked clothes in shock. I am literally wet to the bone. Obviously thinking the same thing, Aidan lets out a stunned laugh.

'Mel was always a joker. I guess this is her last prank...'

I join in with his laughter and run my fingers through my wet hair. 'Well, she got us good!'

Another flash of lightning shoots across the sky in the distance and Aidan looks out of the windscreen sceptically. 'This isn't looking promising for the drive back.' He muses, as the thunderous rain pelts down on the roof the car.

'Maybe it will pass quickly.' Digging my phone out of my pocket to check the forecast, I frown when I realise I don't have a signal. 'Maybe we should sit it out?'

'I guess we could. It is rush hour.' His jacket drips wet splodges onto his damp jeans as he brushes back his sopping hair. 'Are you not in a hurry to get back?'

'Not at all.' I shake my head in response and attempt to dry my phone with the lining of my handbag. 'Aldo has Mateo for the day, so I have nothing to rush back for.'

Aidan raises his eyebrows as a smile plays on the corner of his lips. 'You have a cat-sitter?'

'Yes.' I reply confidently, not realising he's poking fun at me until it's too late. 'I don't like Mateo to be alone.'

'What do you want to do to pass the time?' Aidan raps his knuckles on the steering wheel and looks deep in thought. 'I'll be honest and say there's not much to do in this area. Apart from a country pub back there, we're pretty much in the middle of nowhere.'

I catch a glimpse of my bedraggled appearance in the window and scowl. 'Do you think they'll let us in like this?'

'Well, there's only one way to find out...'

Chapter 28

Warming my hands on my coffee mug, I laugh along as Aidan tells me all about his life with Mel. For the past couple of hours, we have talked about everything. From how the pair of them met, to their tropical wedding day and their home life here in Surrey. We've laughed, we've cried, but more importantly, we have talked about things that just this morning seemed utterly impossible. Aidan has come back to life. Coming here and facing what he was too afraid to do has reawakened him. His eyes are brighter, his smile is deeper and his laugh finally sounds genuine. It's fascinating to see and I feel honoured to have witnessed this turning point in his life.

'Would you like another coffee?' Aidan asks, draining his cup and pointing to my near-empty mug.

Glancing out of the window, I screw up my nose as I realise the rain is still pounding against the walls of the building. 'I guess one more won't hurt.'

Aidan smiles happily and heads over to the bar, giving me the opportunity to escape to the bathroom. Grabbing my handbag, I push out my chair and slip through the cluster of tables. The toilets are exactly like the rest of the pub. Rustic, retro, but with that touch of glamour that brings it all together beautifully. Pausing to check out my reflection, I let out a gasp as I take in the woman staring back at me. Black mascara rings sit beneath my eyes and my hair, which is still damp and slightly curly from the rain, is clinging to my cheeks in the most unflattering manner. Thankfully, my clothes have had the decency to dry out, but my skin still feels cold and clammy.

After breathing some life back into my dishevelled appearance, I quickly use the facilities and head back into the pub. Finding Aidan silently watching the rain pound against the pavement, I drop my handbag under the table as a loud bang erupts above our heads.

'I haven't seen weather like this in years...' I marvel, joining him by the window.

'Neither have I, but we should really be setting off if we have any hope of making it back at a reasonable hour.'

I glance down at my watch and frown as I realise it is almost nine o'clock in the evening.

'There's been a report of a crash on the M25.' The barman pipes up behind us.

Aidan's smile momentarily freezes at the word *crash* and I pretend that I haven't noticed.

'They're advising against all but essential travel until the storm passes.'

Spinning around, I smile in response as the chatty barman places two fresh coffee mugs on our table.

'We do have rooms left if you want to spend the night and sit it out?' He adds, grabbing the empty cups and leaving a dinner menu in their place.

'We've been sitting it out for the past few hours.' I point to our wet clothing and let out a laugh.

'Well, if the forecast is anything to go by, the storm isn't going anywhere until morning. Either way, let me know.' With a friendly smile, the barman scuttles off to another table.

'What do you think?' I ask, once he is out of earshot. 'Do you really think it is that bad out there?'

Yet another bang confirms to me that it is.

Pulling out a chair, I take a seat and bring the coffee mug towards me. 'I guess it *is* pretty dangerous to drive through a storm when we could just stay here and head back first thing in the morning.'

'Are you sure you don't mind?' Aidan sighs and rubs his face agitatedly.

'Honestly, it's fine. These things happen. Let me just call Aldo and let him know.' Grabbing my phone, I walk to a secluded corner of the bar and try to get a signal.

After a few unsuccessful attempts at calling, I resort to sending a text message. It won't go through right now, but hopefully it will deliver as soon as I pick up a signal.

Returning to our table, I smile at Aidan and pick up my coffee. 'I couldn't get though, but it's only a matter of hours and we will be on our way again. It's no big deal in the grand scheme of things.'

'Thank you, Sadie.' Aidan rests his elbows on the table and runs his finger over the rim of his cup. 'I know I've already said this, but I will never be able to thank you enough and I don't just mean for today. You gave me your time when no one else would. You took it upon yourself to help me when I was a complete stranger. If it wasn't for you, I would still be in that state. You saved me without even realising it and I'll never forget it.'

Brushing off his kind words, I try to hide my pink cheeks behind my mug. Inside, my heart is beaming with pride. I knew all he needed was someone to give him the time of day and break down the walls he had built up around him.

'You're more than welcome. It's my job to help people.' Clinking my mug against his, I take a sip and place it on the table. 'So, where's next for Aidan Wilder?'

Aidan looks deep in thought and shrugs his shoulders. 'I don't know, but I know that I don't want to stay in Surrey. It's not my home anymore and coming here has enabled me to make peace with that. When I was by the stream, I could almost hear Mel telling me to go and see the world. To live life and to embrace every moment. I want to see the things she didn't get to see and do the things she didn't get to do. The idea of travelling is suddenly so appealing to me.'

I smile, half happy for him and half sad for myself. As much as I've tried to deny it, I have become very fond of Aidan. We've connected on a level that very few other people can do. Even though he's only been in my life for a short period of time, I feel as though I've known him forever. The realisation that the time has come for us to part ways makes my heart sink.

'Where will you go first?' Pulling my sleeves over my hands, I look out of the window to see that the rain is still coming down strong.

'I'm not too sure. Mel always wanted to visit New Zealand. Maybe that would be a good place to start.'

Sadness hits my stomach as I realise he plans to fly to the other side of the world.

'She went through a phase of obsessing over Lake Wanaka. I would catch her on the computer, mapping trails and checking flight prices...'

Listening to Aidan chat animatedly about Mel, I try to put things into perspective. I was warned about getting too attached in training, but this is the first time I have really struggled with the professional boundary. Aidan is a member of the support group and I am his counsellor. Nothing more and nothing less, but I don't want to wave goodbye to him. I don't want our friendship to end here. I want to see him flourish on his journey back to happiness and to continue to be the friend that I've enjoyed being these past few weeks.

Realising my attachment to Aidan isn't healthy, I decide to nip this in the bud. My fondness for him is only going to hurt me in the long run. I've already gone above and beyond the call of duty in coming down here today and this is where it has to end. Aidan is now ready to put this period of his life behind him and move on. My job here is done.

I don't believe that many things are meant to be, but I do believe that Aidan was meant to come into my life. The stars aligned for our paths to cross, but as Ruby once told me, not everyone who comes into your life is supposed to stay.

Knowing what I have to do, I wait for him to pause before letting out a forced yawn. 'I'm exhausted. It's been a pretty eventful day.'

Aidan nods and stifles a yawn of his own. 'Sorry if I've bored you with my rambling. It just feels so good to have that weight lifted from my shoulders.'

'Honestly, it's fine. It's been an absolute pleasure.' Grabbing my handbag, I tug on my jacket and glance at my watch, signalling that I'm ready to leave.

Aidan opens his mouth to say something, but swiftly closes it and pushes away his mug. 'I'll go and get a couple of rooms.'

Ignoring the growing sadness in my stomach, I smile sadly in response and watch him walk away. Taking the opportunity to check my phone, I jiggle it about in a lame attempt at locating a signal. Eventually resorting to taking the battery out and putting it back in again, I look up as Aidan returns with two room cards.

'Are you ready?' He asks, hovering by the table as I quickly click the battery back into the handset.

Standing up, I quickly check that we haven't left anything behind and follow Aidan up the short flight of stairs. Coming to a stop in front of two rooms at the far end of a corridor, Aidan checks the cards before handing one to me.

'You're in Room Seven. I hope it's okay for you. It's not luxury, but...'

'I'm sure it will be fine.' I take the card from him gratefully and slip it into the reader. 'Goodnight, Aidan.'

Pushing my way inside, I am about to let the door swing shut behind me when Aidan shouts out.

'Sadie?'

Sticking my head out into the lobby, my heart races as he stares back at me.

'You're the kindest person I have ever met. If it wasn't for you, I would still be that empty shell of a man. Wallowing, deteriorating and letting life pass me by. I'll never forget what about you have done for me.'

We stare at one another, the silence between us saying everything that I could ever wish to say.

'Goodnight, Aidan...'

Throwing open the curtains, I marvel at the clear blue skies ahead. All traces of the torrential downpour last night have been washed away and in their place is the start of a beautiful day. Captivated by the early birds, who are harmoniously chirping in the forest, I almost don't hear the gentle knocking. Tearing myself away from the stunning view, I open the door to reveal Aidan.

'Sleep well?' He asks, as I reach for my handbag and follow him out into the lobby.

'Yes.' I lie, glossing over the fact that I tossed and turned for hours on end. 'Did you?'

'I honestly did. For the first time in as long as I can remember, I slept straight through the night.' He smiles broadly and I automatically return it.

'That's great.' Taking care not to trip on the steep steps, we make our way downstairs. 'I'm really pleased to hear it.'

Leaving Aidan to return the room cards to the bar, I push my way outside and hover by the car. Locating my phone at the bottom of my bag, I let out a relieved sigh as I discover I finally have a signal again. Tapping the screen, I squint to get my eyes to focus as a bunch of missed call notifications flash up on the display. Hitting voicemail, I press the handset to my ear and smile as Ruby's familiar voice floods out of the speakers.

Sadie!
I've been trying to call you all night!
I'm going to Jamaica... tomorrow!
The September trip was fully booked, but there
was a slot with the Congleton branch.
It's super last-minute, so I haven't had the chance
to think if I'm doing the right thing.
If I can get the courage to go through with it, I will
be flying at two from Terminal One.
I could really do with your advice.
Please call me!

Staring at the phone in shock, I frantically tap the keypad in a panicked bid to call her. The line seems to ring out forever before clicking over to voicemail. Immediately hitting redial, I glance at my watch and feel a surge of panic when I realise it's almost seven.

'Is everything okay?' Aidan asks, clearly recognising the panicked expression on my face as he beeps open the car.

'I need to get back...' My voice trails off as I press the handset to my ear once more. 'Come on! Pick up!' I groan, drumming my fingers on the bonnet of the car impatiently.

Aidan flashes me a questioning look as I throw my arms in the air in frustration.

'How long will it take to get back to Cheshire?' I stammer, opening the door and hastily fastening my seatbelt.

'Around four hours. If we're lucky, we will make it in three.' Getting the hint there's not a second to waste, he dives into the car and turns over the engine. 'What's going on?'

'I've got to get the airport. My friend is flying at two and I need to see her before she leaves.' Quickly typing out a message, I divert my attention to Aldo as Aidan puts his foot down.

When he doesn't pick up either, I scratch my nose in confusion.

'Is she going anywhere nice?' Aidan asks, covering his mouth as he yawns.

'She's going to the Caribbean for a couple of months.' I explain, logging onto my Twitter account and sending Ruby a message on there, too. 'She works for a travel agency. They're sending her on a tour of their top resorts.'

'Wow. That sounds incredible.' Aidan gushes, clearly impressed.

'I know, but she suffers from anxiety, so this is a huge deal for her. If it wasn't for me pestering her, she wouldn't be going at all. I'll never forgive myself if I don't make it back in time...'

'Don't worry, there shouldn't be any traffic at this time on a Sunday.' Giving me a reassuring smile, he presses the accelerator.

As Aidan strives to get us home at record speed, I clutch my phone to my chest and replay Ruby's message in my mind. She's actually going! I can't quite believe it. I could kick myself for being so far away right now. I should be with her. I should be egging her on and helping her to pack. We should be painting our nails and chatting excitedly about all of the amazing things she is going to see. Instead, I am almost two hundred miles away, wearing slept-in clothes in a last-minute dash to the airport.

Biting my nail anxiously, I glance over at Aidan and immediately feel guilty. I shouldn't feel bad for coming to Surrey. Helping him through this has been my biggest achievement since becoming a counsellor.

'Thank you for inviting me down here.' I mumble, suddenly remembering how important this trip was. 'It was truly an honour for me.'

'You have nothing to thank me for. As I said last night, I will never be able to repay you for helping me to get back on my feet. You have been my guardian angel.'

Aidan's eyes crinkle into a smile and I feel my stomach flip. Remembering the promise I made to myself last night, I clear my throat and change the subject.

'So, how long do you think you will spend in New Zealand?' I ask, turning to look out of the window.

We come to a set of traffic lights and Aidan brakes gently. 'I don't know. There's not really anything to come back for, so there's nothing to stop me from staying there indefinitely.'

'Wow…' The word *indefinitely* hits me like a punch to the stomach as I nod in response. 'Well, wherever you end up in the world, I wish you a lifetime of happiness.'

There's a strange silence as we turn onto the motorway, before Aidan flicks on the radio to fill it.

'And where do you think *you* will end up?' He eventually asks, searching through the music channels.

I turn in my seat to face him and frown in confusion. 'Alderley Edge. Blossom View is my home.'

'Do you see yourself there forever?'

I pause for a moment, considering his question carefully. I've never really put much thought into my long-term future before. I tend to think month to month, not year to year. I close my eyes and try to imagine my life elsewhere. I can't see myself in the Spanish sun, eating tapas on a terracotta terrace. Nor do I believe I will be singing the American National Anthem anytime soon and I'm positive that throwing on a backpack and exploring Brazil isn't on my radar.

'You know what?' I reply confidently, unable to hide my growing smile. 'I think Cheshire is exactly where my future lies. I love my job, I love my home and I love my village. I don't think there's a place in the world I would rather be.'

Aidan nods along and returns my smile. 'To be safe in the knowledge that you know exactly what your future holds must be an amazing feeling.'

'That's a different thing entirely.' I interrupt, wagging my finger at him. 'I know where it *lies*, but I am completely clueless as to what it holds.'

'Would you want to know?' He asks, swiftly changing lanes. 'If you could see how your life would pan out, would you want to know?'

Shaking my head, I stare out at the open road ahead and relax my eyes.

'In my experience, the only way to go through life is by taking it one day at a time. Live in the moment, have no regrets and embrace everything that life throws at you, because you'll never know the value of a moment, until it becomes a memory...'

Chapter 30

'No!' I exclaim, shaking my phone in anger as the battery decides to give up the fight. 'This cannot be happening!'

Quickly attempting to turn it back on, I jab at the keyboard in frustration. After three long hours and thirty tiring minutes of sporadic text messages and unanswered calls, my phone has finally died.

'Don't panic.' Following the signs for Manchester Airport, Aidan presses the accelerator. 'We're literally five minutes away.'

Trying to take his advice, I tap my foot impatiently. With a stroke of luck and a smidge of expert driving, we managed to make it back to Cheshire in just under four hours. Ruby's flight hasn't left yet, if she hasn't checked-in, we should just about make it.

'Do you know which terminal she is flying from?' Aidan asks, studying the brightly-coloured signs by the roundabout.

'One...' I mumble, not certain at all if that's correct.

Indicating left, Aidan puts his foot down as we head towards the departures drop-off point. Placing my hand over the seatbelt buckle, I wait until he comes to a swift stop before releasing the clasp and throwing open the door.

'I'll wait right here!' Aidan yells after me, as I tear into the airport and look around the crowded building for Ruby.

Not being able to locate her in the swarms of people, I dash to the information board and scan the list for the next flight to Jamaica. The letters change before my eyes, reeling off a whole new bunch of destinations. Spotting Sangster Airport, I dodge a group of gaggling girls and charge across the tiles to the designated check-in desk. Sprinting to the counter, I gasp for breath and rap my knuckles on the desk to get the assistant's attention.

'Excuse me?' I gabble. 'Has Ruby Robinson checked-in yet?'

Turning around, the smiling assistant abandons her paperwork and takes a step towards me. 'I'm sorry?'

'I'm looking for my friend.' I explain, taking a quick look over my shoulder for her. 'She's on this flight to Jamaica. Can you tell me if she has checked-in yet, please?'

Smiling apologetically, she shakes her head of blonde curls. 'I'm so sorry, but I can't tell you that information.'

Frowning in dismay, I hold my head in my hands and groan as she moves over to her computer and clacks at the keyboard.

'Although, I *can* tell you that one person is yet to check-in for this flight and there are still another thirty minutes until check-in closes.' She winks discreetly, before turning her attention to the next person in line.

Breathing a sigh of relief, I move aside and try to get my eyes to focus on the hundreds of people around me. There's no chance of finding her in here. It's like trying to locate a needle in a haystack. Spinning around, I weave my way to the window and perch on the railing sadly. Rubbing my throbbing temples, I close my eyes and consider giving up, when I hear a familiar voice in the distance.

Standing on the tips of my toes to pinpoint the sound in the buzzing blanket of people, I spot two heads of aubergine waves walking my way. Rushing over, my lips stretch into a relieved smile as I come to a stop in front of them.

'Sadie!' Ruby exclaims, abandoning her suitcase and throwing her arms around my neck. 'Where the hell have you been?'

Quickly smoothing down my slept-in outfit, I tuck my hair behind my ears. 'I went to Surrey... I was only supposed to be there for a few hours... but then it rained and the lightning was so bad... we decided to stay the night... there was no signal, so I only received your messages in the morning... I tried to call, but my battery died and...'

'Slow down!' Ruby laughs and puts her hand on my shoulder. 'You're here now. That's the main thing.'

I look at my dear friend and feel my heart swell with pride. She looks so happy, so vibrant and so full of life. The whole way here I envisaged her panicked, scared and worried, but I couldn't have been more wrong. The young woman in front of me is positively glowing. Frank might have tormented Ruby over her decision to do this, but right now, he is nowhere to be seen.

Too busy fawning over Ruby's glowing demeanour, I almost don't realise I haven't given Yvette a second glance. Turning my attention to Ruby's mother, I attempt a friendly smile, but stop myself when I see she doesn't look happy in the slightest.

'Isn't this incredible?' I gush, pointing to Ruby and beaming brightly. 'What an amazing adventure she is about to embark on!'

Yvette mumbles in agreement and rolls her eyes. 'Come on, let's get this charade over with.'

Ruby bites her lip and I notice a wave of hurt wash across her face. 'I'll go and check-in.'

Watching Ruby tentatively take her passport out of her bag, I wait until she's out of earshot before pulling Yvette to one side.

'Would it kill you to be a little bit supportive?' I hiss, unable to disguise the anger that is rising in my throat.

Yvette's face freezes and she folds her arms defensively. 'Excuse me?'

'This is a *huge* deal for her...'

'Why are you making such a big deal out of this?' Yvette scowls and shakes her head. 'It's a free trip to the Caribbean.'

'You just don't get it, do you?' I stare at Yvette's surly face, completely flummoxed by her dismissive attitude. 'Ruby's anxiety makes even the smallest task seem impossible. The fact that she's brave enough to get on that plane, not knowing *if* or *when* she will have an anxiety attack is a huge step for her. She has faith in herself that she can take this on, why can't you?'

Choosing to reply with a shrug of her shoulders, Yvette stifles a yawn.

I usually feel sorry for people who misjudge mental health sufferers. After all, it's not their fault they don't understand how matters of the mind work, but Yvette just makes me mad. Ruby has been a victim of anxiety for years and not once has she bothered to educate herself on exactly what her daughter is going through.

'Do you know what it's like to have anxiety, Yvette?' I ask, using every ounce of energy I have to stop myself from losing my temper. 'To wake up every day in the hope that this will be the day you're freed from the fear that causes your stomach to churn uncontrollably?'

Refusing to respond, she purses her lips and looks away.

'Ruby has come so far on her journey with her mental health, but she still struggles on a daily basis. Even the slightest thing can send her right back to where she was a few years ago...'

'We gave Ruby a lovely life.' Yvette interjects angrily, taking a step towards me. 'She had an upbringing most children could only dream of. There's absolutely no reason for Ruby to have *anxiety...*'

'Anxiety doesn't work like that. There's not always a tragedy in someone's life that causes them to have anxiety, depression, panic attacks or any other mental ailment.' I explain, keeping my voice low to ensure the people next to us don't hear. 'But the thing that the majority of sufferers I encounter have in common, is a family who doesn't understand.'

Yvette's stony exterior stays firmly in place, but I notice a flicker of guilt in her eyes.

'Anxiety can seem impossible to understand if you've never experienced it, but if you make the effort to educate yourself, even just a little bit, it will help your relationship with your daughter immensely.' I place my hand on her arm and notice her visibly flinch at my touch. 'I know what it's like to have a mother who doesn't understand, Yvette. Yes, Ruby has the support group and she has me, but what she really needs is her mum.'

Before I can say another word, Ruby returns with her boarding pass and looks between the two of us uneasily. 'Is everything okay?'

I glance at Yvette and hold my breath, hoping beyond hope that she has had a change in attitude.

'Everything's fine.' Yvette breathes, her cheeks flushing violently as she avoids making eye contact with either of us. 'I might not say it very often, but I'm so proud of you, Ruby.'

My gaze flits to Ruby and I see her jaw drop open as she stares at her mother in shock.

'I've made no secret of the fact I don't understand your anxiety, but that doesn't mean I don't care.' Yvette's voice wobbles and she disguises it by clearing her throat. 'If at any point you feel like you're not happy out there, just get back on that plane and I'll be right here waiting for you when get off at the other end.'

Ruby's eyes become glassy and I tactfully take a step back, not wanting to impose on their tender moment. Embracing one another warmly, Yvette kisses Ruby on the cheek as an announcement booms out of the airport speakers.

This is the final boarding call for Flight SCC137 to Jamaica.
Can all remaining passengers please go to Gate 17 immediately.

'That's me...' Ruby says excitedly, reaching out for her suitcase.

Smiling back at her, I let out a squeal as she hugs me tightly.

'Thank you so much for making me do this.' She whispers into my ear. 'If it wasn't for you, I never would have had the courage to actually go through with it.'

Shaking my head, I smooth down her curls. 'You've always had the courage, Ruby. You just had to find it for yourself.'

We lock eyes and I feel a lump form in my throat as yet another announcement fills the air.

Gate 17 is now closing.
Can all remaining passengers please make their way to the gate.

'Go!' I instruct, shooing her away joyfully. 'You're going to miss your flight!'

Nodding in response, Ruby hugs her mum one last time before taking her suitcase and walking towards the escalator.

'See you soon!' I yell after her, cupping my hands around my mouth. 'Have a fabulous time!'

I look over at Yvette as we watch Ruby step onto the escalator. Beaming proudly, she waves her arms around in the air until Ruby disappears out of sight.

'This trip is going to be so good for her.' I gush, giving Yvette a friendly squeeze. 'The independence, the change of environment and the freedom will give her a whole new lease of life.'

'I hope so.' Yvette nods and smiles back at me. 'I really, really do...'

Chapter 31

For a short while, we both stand perfectly still, glued to the spot as a strange buzz hangs in the air between us.

'You're always welcome to come along to the Anxiety Anonymous meetings.' I mumble, staring at the empty escalator in a proud daze. 'Counselling can be just as beneficial for the families of sufferers.'

Yvette screws up her nose and frowns. 'I don't think it's for me. I'm not really good at... *talking* to people like that.'

'You don't need to say a single word.' I explain, as we start to make our way towards the exit. 'Just sitting in the background and listening to the others will help you to understand what anxiety really is.'

'Maybe.' Yvette replies apprehensively. 'I'll think about it, but I don't want to promise anything.'

'Just thinking about it is a great start.' Heaping on the praise in the hope that she takes the bait, I feel around in my pocket and hand her an Anxiety Anonymous business card. 'Anytime you want to join us, you know where we are.'

Reluctantly accepting the glossy card, she slips it into her handbag as we step outside into the sunshine. I consider inviting her for a spot of lunch, but with a final smile Yvette heads towards the car park, leaving me on the pavement alone.

'Did you find her?' Aidan yells out of the car window, piercing my thought bubble and bringing me back to reality.

I turn around and smile to myself as I realise Aidan is in the exact same spot where I left him earlier. His dark eyes crinkle into a smile as I nod in response and slowly walk over to him. If saying goodbye to one friend wasn't bad enough, now I have to do it all over again with Aidan.

'Are you okay?' He asks, giving me a cautious glance and hesitating before starting the engine.

'I'm fine.' I reply, almost curtly, hoping he takes this as a signal I'm ready to leave.

Taking the hint that I'm not in the mood for making idle chit-chat, he releases the handbrake in silence. As we leave the airport behind and start to make our way towards Alderley Edge, my stomach starts to churn and I'm not too sure it's solely due to the lack of sleep. There's an elephant in the room, which neither of us wants to address and that's mainly because we don't really know what it is.

As we get closer to home, the car seems to slow down to a snail's pace until we eventually come to a stop outside Blossom View. Looking out of the window, I stare at my beautiful cottage, not moving a muscle. I should be itching to get in there. I should be relieved to get out of yesterday's clothes and into my own bed, but something is stopping me. Something doesn't want me to get out of this car and if I really listen to my instincts, it's because I know that this is it. Once I walk through that door, I probably won't see him again. Our journey stops right here. This is where our time together ends.

Reluctantly picking up my handbag, I unclip my seatbelt and reach for the door handle, not daring to look directly at Aidan.

'Thank you so much, Sadie.' He mumbles, a tone to his voice I haven't heard before.

'You've already thanked me.' I whisper sadly, looking down into my lap. 'Besides, it's my job...'

'No, no it's not.' Aidan shakes his head and swivels around in his seat. 'It's not your job to give up your free time. It's not your job to care about a stranger as though they're your own family and it's not your job to be the kindest, most genuine, caring person I have ever met.'

A lump forms in my throat as my bottom lip starts to tremble.

'You don't give yourself enough credit.' Placing his hand on my shoulder, he pulls me towards him. 'The world would be a better place if there were more people like you in it.'

Reaching across the seat, I hug him tightly, not wanting to ever let go. A single tear slips down my cheek, landing in a pool on his shoulder. There's a moment where neither of us breathe a word, the deathly silence speaking volumes.

'So, New Zealand?' I manage, sniffing in a poor bid to compose myself.

'New Zealand.' Aidan confirms quietly, resting his arm on the steering wheel and staring out at the open road. 'And from there, who knows?'

I nod along and resign myself to the fact that it's time to say goodbye. Taking a deep breath, I force myself to smile and grab my bag.

'Goodbye, Aidan.'

Bringing his eyes up to meet mine, he nods and returns my weak attempt at a smile. 'Goodbye, Sadie.'

Stepping out of the car, I hesitate before closing the door. 'If you ever find yourself back in Cheshire, I'll still be here and I'll probably still have a whole lot of building work that needs to be done.'

Aidan nods and looks down at his ring finger as I close the door and begrudgingly walk up the garden path. Sliding my key into the lock, I pause and look over my shoulder. Aidan raises his hand and turns over the engine, clearly waiting for me to step inside before he leaves. Waving back at him, I ignore the sadness in my stomach and step inside, allowing the door to close with a thud behind me.

Leaning against the wall, I stand frozen to the spot, not really knowing what to do with myself. Eventually hearing the car pull away, I force myself to wander into the living room and hit the flashing button on the answering machine. Aldo's angry voice floods into the room and I collapse onto the couch as I listen to the many frustrated voicemails. Before I have the chance to hit *redial,* there's a knock at the door.

A frisson of adrenaline rushes through me as I realise it could be Aidan. Pulling open the door, my smile vanishes as I see Aldo standing there and not Aidan as I'd hoped.

'Where the hell have you been?' He demands, picking up a cat crate from the floor and pushing past me. 'I've been going out of my mind with worry!'

'I'm so sorry...' I begin, unlocking the crate and freeing Mateo to pad around the living room.

'Sorry isn't good enough!' Aldo booms, folding his arms angrily.

'Didn't you get my text message?' Pulling Mateo onto my lap, I curl up into a ball and flick on the television. 'I tried to call you...'

'Yes, I got the bloody message... at *seven* this morning! I was awake all night worrying about you! I nearly called the police!' Pacing up and down around the living room, he throws his arms in the air dramatically. 'I knew it was a bad idea going down there with that creep. I *knew* it...'

'Will you calm down, please?' I groan, rubbing my tired eyes. 'We had some car trouble, so we were already delayed and then the storm came in. There was no signal in the forest, hence why I couldn't contact you, but look, I'm safe, there's no harm done.'

'You do know you've missed Ruby, don't you?' He retorts, tapping his freshly-manicured nails on the fireplace. 'She was devastated when she couldn't get in touch with you.'

'I've seen her. I went straight to the airport as soon as I received her messages.' I explain, hoping this will calm him down an iota.

'Oh...' Aldo narrows his eyes at me and throws his hair over his shoulder. 'Anyway, I don't like you going off with random men like that. Please don't make a habit of it.'

Kicking off my shoes, I cross my legs and run my fingers through Mateo's fur. 'There's no reason to worry about that, because Aidan's gone. I won't be seeing him again.'

Aldo frowns and takes a seat next to me. 'Well, that's good to know as you have your date with Pierce on Friday and five days isn't long to get you ready to meet the man of your dreams.'

I smile back at him nervously, my interest in this date is pretty much non-existent.

'I'm going to come over on Thursday and get you ready. I'm talking nails, hair, facial...'

As Aldo rambles off his plans to make me date-worthy, I find my mind wandering back to Surrey. To the chat on the embankment, to the magical moment in the forest, to the babbling brook and to the laughter in the pub. Aidan has set himself free. He's finally detached himself from the grief that was destroying his life, so why am I not happy for him? Why do I feel so empty and hollow? And more worryingly, why do I feel as though I've lost him, when he wasn't mine to keep...

Chapter 32

Looking at the release cushion as it is passed around the circle, I smile at Alec as he accepts the red pillow from the woman on his left.

'Believe it or not, I actually have something good to say today.' Sitting up straight, his eyes sparkle as he speaks.

'As many of you know, I've struggled with anxiety and depression for such a long time. Most of my ups and downs have been discussed in this very room. It's no secret that there have been more downs than ups, but this week I am feeling good.'

He pauses and takes a sip from his bottle of water.

'We're always so quick to take the cushion and pour our hearts out about how terrible we have been feeling, but many of us seem to keep quiet about the times when we feel well.'

Intrigued by his point, I lean forward in my seat and nod along as Alec explains further.

'Anxiety often comes over me with no warning and this week, I have experienced a similar thing. But instead of the crippling worry, I have been hit with an inexplicable sense of being carefree.'

A small round of applause erupts and he waits for it to subside before continuing.

'Just to be clear, I'm not implying that I'm now free of anxiety. My point is, instead of taking the moments where we're feeling good for granted, we should grasp them with both hands and cherish every second.'

Another round of applause starts up and this time, I join in.

'Alec has raised a fabulous point here. We are all aware that anxiety comes in waves, but so many of us focus only on the bad times and totally discount the good. However, the good times are an example of our control over anxiety.' I shift around to get comfortable and smile at the faces staring back at me.

'When we feel at our lowest, all our memories of the times where we have felt perfectly fine evaporate, but as Alec has just said, we should *always* remember our good days. These times remind us that the anxiety we're experiencing is only temporary. It has passed us before and it will pass again. No one feeling is permanent.'

A lady in red at the far end of the circle raises her hand and I motion for her to speak up.

'I started to realise that I only turned to my diary when I was struggling and as a result, it was filled with sadness and negativity. Tiring of flicking through page after page of bad memories, I decided to buy myself another diary.'

Reaching into her handbag, she pulls out two identical notepads, one red and one silver.

'When I have had a good day, I write in the silver and when anxiety hits, I write in the red. Now, when I'm feeling down, I will grab the silver diary and read through all the good times I've had. Just reminding myself that things will get better gives me hope that the anxiety isn't forever.'

A few people mutter in agreement and I silently remark at how true that is.

'Separating the good days from the bad has also helped me to recognise what triggers my anxiety. More often than not, triggers aren't always clear to see when you're under a cloud. I've found it extremely useful to look back over my notes when I'm in the right frame of mind and assess them clearly. Sometimes, it's only when we take a step back that we can see what was right in front of us all along.'

Completely lost in her words, I almost don't realise people are waiting for me to speak. Hastily clearing my throat, I snap back to the task at hand.

'Diaries are another great idea and something which we should discuss in further detail at the next meeting.' I reply, quickly realising that we're almost out of time. 'Unfortunately, our time is almost up...'

Alec coughs and raises his hand to interject. 'Sadie, can I ask you a question before we leave?'

'Of course.' I raise my eyebrows at him and smile. 'You can ask me anything.'

Alec studies my face carefully and frowns. 'How are *you?* Day after day, we sit here and you ask us how we're doing. You listen whilst we pour our hearts out to you, but we never ask how you are.'

Touched by his kind thought, I lick my dry lips and shake my head. 'It doesn't really work that way...'

'Well, today it does.' He smiles and passes me the release cushion. 'I'm not asking you as our counsellor. I'm asking you as our friend.'

My heart swells as I look around the room of people who I've become so fond of.

'I'm okay.' I reply, forcing myself to smile back at them. 'I'm doing really...'

Hearing the words slip out of my mouth, I realise I'm doing the exact opposite of what I encourage these brave people to do. I'm lying. I'm putting on a front to hide how I'm really feeling.

'You know what?' I take a deep breath and feel my shoulders become instantly lighter. 'I'm actually feeling a little rubbish today, but just like you guys, I am still here. I am still fighting and I live to face another day.'

'What has triggered you into feeling low?' Alec presses, listening intently to my every word.

'I'm not too sure.' I reply, as an image of Aidan jumps into my mind. 'I guess I'm just having a bad day.'

Suddenly feeling rather uncomfortable at having the tables turned on me, I glance at my watch and stand up.

'Thank you all for coming. Don't forget about the forum if you find yourselves struggling before the next meeting.'

The majority of people in the room stand to their feet and start chatting amongst themselves, but Alec stares at me seemingly unconvinced.

'Have you ever made an unhappiness list?' He asks, plucking my jacket from the back of my seat and holding it out.

'An unhappiness list?' I repeat in confusion, accepting the denim jacket from him.

Alec nods and follows me into the lobby. 'You make a list of everything in your life that makes you unhappy and then you decide how to rectify it.' He explains, straightening out his collar. 'So many people make bucket lists. They have list after list detailing all the things they need in order to make them happy, but they rarely take a moment to recognise the things they already have that make them *un*happy. More often than not, you will realise what you *do* want in your life, by removing what you *don't*.'

I nod along and lean against the information stand. 'Thanks, Alec. That's definitely food for thought.'

With a final wink, he picks up his briefcase and disappears into the car park. Lost in my own thoughts, I wait for the rest of the group to leave before making my way outside. My bucket list must be one of the shortest in history, so why does it feel so unattainable? Delving into the depths of my handbag, I finally locate the tatty piece of paper beneath a mountain of chewing gum wrappers. Smoothing down the corners, I take in the words on the page. *Be happy*. It's just two little words, but those two words hold so much meaning.

Tapping the paper against my fingers, I wonder what is preventing me from feeling as though I've achieved my one goal in life. What is standing in my way and more importantly, what's missing?

Chapter 33

Tapping my pen against the notepad, I take a sip of wine and frown at the blank page in front of me. An unhappiness list sounds so simple in theory, but I haven't been able to come up with a single point. Does that mean my life is perfect? Moonlight floods into the kitchen, illuminating my makeshift desk in a bright light as I chew over that very question. I can think of a million things that *do* make me happy. Blossom View, Mateo, Aldo, Ruby, my job, but what makes me unhappy is a different story.

Swirling wine around my glass, I watch Mateo paw the rug and rack my brains for the last time I felt deeply unhappy. The day I bumped into my mother and told her I loved her made me feel pretty awful. Telling anyone you love them and not hearing it back with meaning always hurts, but when it's your own mother, the pain goes much deeper. Would I be a happier person if my mum and I had a better relationship? I pause for a moment, before writing *mum* on the paper.

Taking the notepad with me, I stroll into the living room and collapse onto the couch with my wine. My gaze lands on the patch of damp in the corner and I recall Aidan's advice.

Ignoring the problem is just intensifying the problem. The longer you leave it, the worse it will become.

Adding *damp* to my list, I come to the conclusion I don't really have anything to feel sad about. On paper, things are going rather well. I have a great job, I've just bought a beautiful home and I have fabulous friends. The emptiness I am feeling just doesn't make any sense. What is missing from my life to fill the sudden void inside me?

Abandoning the unhappiness list, I push myself up as my phone rings in the kitchen. Peering at the screen, my lips spring into a smile as I see Ruby's name flashing back at me. Hitting the green icon, I let out a gasp as the display springs to life.

'Hi!' Ruby exclaims, pushing her sunglasses into her hair and waving at the screen manically. 'Check this out...'

'Oh, my goodness!' I breathe, clasping my hands over my mouth in awe.

The sparkling blue ocean dances under the bright sunshine, creating a dazzling display on the horizon behind her.

'The beaches here are insane!' Reaching down, she grabs a handful of sand and lets it fall through her fingers like powder.

'I can see that!' I reply, laughing at how excited she is. 'Are you having a good time?'

'I'm having an *amazing* time!' Diving onto a sun lounger, she positions her handset into the sand. 'It's better than I ever imagined.'

'I'm so happy to hear that you're enjoying yourself.' Tears prick at the corners of my eyes as my heart fills with pride. 'I knew you would. You just had to have the confidence to believe in yourself...'

Ruby smiles knowingly and turns to look at the turquoise water. 'I did have a slight wobble on the plane, but I managed to shake it off pretty quickly.'

'You should remember that as an example of your control over Frank.' I reply proudly. 'If you ever have a moment of uncertainty, just think back to that time on the plane.'

She adjusts her swimsuit and nods in response. 'I've told the other guys on the trip about my anxiety and they've all been so lovely about it...'

As Ruby proceeds to tell me about her new friends, I marvel at the remarkable change in her. This, right now, is evidence of just how well counselling works and how anxiety *can* be beaten. Just six months ago, Ruby had never contemplated following her dreams. The overpowering fear of anxiety put a firm halt on any plans she dared to make, but despite Frank's attempts at sabotaging her trip, she is living her life to the full.

Just like Aidan, she has had that life-changing moment. She's embracing the world rather than hiding from it. The turning point where you decide your fears aren't going to control you anymore is pivotal for any sufferer. So many of us allow our anxiety to keep us in a box, too afraid to step out of it for fear of what might happen. When the truth is, *nothing* will happen. We just need to find the courage within us to take that leap of faith and break free.

'We're all going down to the local fish fry tonight!' Ruby squeals, allowing the warm water to wash over her toes. 'They have music, local produce and dancing! Isn't that cool?'

'Very cool.' I smile back at her as someone shouts her name in the distance.

Covering the speaker with her hand, she motions for to them to leave her on the beach.

'Go and enjoy yourself!' I giggle, finishing my wine in one swift gulp. 'It's about time I was heading for bed, anyway.'

Scrambling to her feet, she shakes the sand out of her hair and slips on her sunglasses. 'Okay, but I'll call again in a couple of days.'

Waving goodbye, she blows a kiss at the screen and races along the shore as the display bounces to black. For a while, I lean against the counter, a lovely warmth whooshing through my veins from speaking to Ruby. Seeing people kick anxiety to the kerb is my favourite part of the job and it gets better each and every time it happens.

Again, my mind drifts to Aidan and I find myself hoping he's having the same success as Ruby. Is he at The Shepard, packing for his trip? Is he up in the sky, mid-flight? Or is he sprawled on a beach, having a drink in memory of Mel? The thought of the last one brings a smile to my face once more.

Wandering into the living room, I look down at my own list to happiness and sigh heavily. Fixing my relationship with my mother and addressing the damp don't sound like major issues, but at least one of those is going to be easier said than done. After all, you can't fix something that doesn't want to be repaired, but at least I will sleep easy at night knowing that I've tried...

Chapter 34

Watching the world go by from the window, I find myself wondering if I am doing the right thing. Thelma's Tea Room makes the perfect location for almost any meeting, but the thought of my mother walking through the door makes me want to hurl. A part of me thinks this impending conversation isn't worth my energy. It's been such a long time since my mum and I had a good relationship that I don't even know where to start.

Carefully blowing into the steaming mug, my smile freezes as my mother steps into the café. Not saying a word, she pulls out a chair at the opposite end of the table and offers me a strained smile. I beam back at her, remarking at how similar we look. Her eyes, her nose, her mouth. Even the laughter lines on her temples are exactly like mine. How can we be so similar, yet so very different?

'So, how are you?' I eventually ask, trying to keep my voice steady.

'Fine.' She retorts, immediately seeming uncomfortable. 'You?'

I nod in response as she orders a coffee with the waiter.

'Well, this is nice.' I say awkwardly, as my stomach does somersaults.

'Yes, it is.' Fiddling with the edge of the menu, she turns to look away.

Regretting my decision to invite her here today, I concentrate on the reason behind this awkward meeting. 'I thought it would be nice if we did this more often.'

My mum flashes me a confused look and purses her lips. 'What do you mean?'

I pause as the waiter returns with a cappuccino and places it in front of her.

'I want us to make more of an effort to get along.' Cradling my mug, I rest my elbows on the table, studying her reaction carefully.

'We *do* get along?' She mutters, totally dismissing my point. 'What are you talking about?'

I stare at my mum and wonder how it got this far. How have we gone from mother and daughter to strangers in just twenty-six years?

'Can we please stop this charade?' I beg, my heart starting to sink. 'It's draining...'

'Look, Sadie.' She interrupts curtly. 'I don't know where this went wrong...'

'It went wrong when you put Mick before me!' I hiss, trying to keep my voice down. 'It went wrong when you washed your hands of me at twenty-one and it went wrong when you ridiculed my struggles with my mental health.'

Her face freezes as she looks around the busy café, completely mortified by my outburst. 'Sadie...'

'No, don't try and brush this under the carpet. We need to sort this out.' Placing my palms face down on the table, I fix my gaze on hers. 'Why do you refuse to talk about the obvious problems we have?'

Shaking her head, she looks down at the ground dejectedly. 'Because I don't know how to fix it...'

'Then try!' I cry, completely exasperated.

'I don't know what to say!' Throwing her arms in the air, her cheeks turn pink as her bottom lip starts to tremble. 'I'm a terrible mother, okay? Is that what you want to hear?'

'No!' I yell, not caring that other people are now staring at us. 'I want to hear how we're going to put this right.'

She holds her head in her hands for what feels like forever, until finally looking up. 'I was never cut out to be a mother, Sadie. You know that more than anyone.'

I nod in response, unable to deny her lack of motherly instincts.

'I struggled so much when you were young, but when the money came through, I thought I could actually make a difference to your life. It's no secret that Mick doesn't like kids, but he's not all bad. He had a rough time as a child, worse than you could ever imagine. He was lucky if he ate, so he can't understand it when people shower their kids with materialistic things.'

Unable to accept her explanation of Mick's awful behaviour, I roll my eyes and look away.

'The fact that you two couldn't get along killed me, so the only way I knew how to deal with it was to keep you apart. As time went on, you drifted further and further away. Yes, I disapprove of your lifestyle choices. I had dreams of you being a doctor, a lawyer or something else academic. You're a bright girl, Sadie. Seeing you dedicate your life to art and counselling seems such a waste to me.'

Hearing her refer to counselling as a *waste* makes my blood boil.

'This is exactly what the problem is.' I retort angrily. 'A good mother doesn't judge and ridicule the things their children are passionate about. A good mother is supportive and encourages you to follow your dreams.'

She drops her head to her chest and lowers her voice to a whisper. 'I know what it's like to follow your passion instead of a strong and stable career. You remember just how much we struggled before. I want more for you than that. Yes, we are financially secure now, but that money won't last forever. I just want you to have a secure future.'

Despite my efforts to keep a stern face, my angry posterior flickers. I can't argue with that. It's no secret that we had nothing when I was growing up. The modest council house we lived in was a far cry from our prestigious village.

'It doesn't feel like you want the best for me. Most of the time, it's like you don't want anything to do with me at all.' Saying this out loud makes my stomach pang with sadness, but the truth always hurts. 'When I was at my lowest, you didn't give me a second thought. I needed a mother then more than ever.'

'I thought you didn't need me.' She protests weakly. 'I thought you were independent and strong-willed...'

'I *had* to be independent and strong-willed.' A lump forms in my throat and I try my best to swallow it. 'I don't have anyone else. I don't have any siblings and you've made no secret of not wanting me to reconnect with my biological father. You're all that I have.'

Seemingly lost for words, she stares at the table as tears silently roll down her face.

'There are no excuses for my behaviour, Sadie. I was wrong and I don't know what to do to put it right.' Her voice trails off into a series of sobs and I feel my jaw drop open at her apology.

There are a million things I want to say to her, but I don't breathe a word. Picking her apart and reminding her of all the times where she's let me down isn't going to help things one iota. If we have any hope of putting this behind us and moving on, we have to draw a line beneath this. We have to leave the past in the past and start to pave the way for a future together.

'What's in the past doesn't matter. What matters now is what we choose to do from here.' Leaning across the table, I hold out my hand for hers.

After initially hesitating, she places her palm in mine. 'I'm so sorry, Sadie.'

For the first time in the history of our relationship, I hear her say those words and actually mean them. Pushing out my chair, I walk around the table and embrace her tightly. Letting the tears fall, I rest my head on her shoulder and allow myself to cry.

Alec was right. We bury the things that make us unhappy so deeply, we don't even acknowledge them anymore. We become so unaware of their existence that we simply accept them and live our lives under a cloud. Today has made me realise that it's not always about trying to fix something that's broken. Sometimes, it's about starting over and creating something infinitely better...

Chapter 35

Picking up a sparkly dress, I run my fingers over the soft fabric before hanging it back on the rail. I'm surrounded by beautiful garments, but not a single one is calling out to me. No matter how hard I try to be seduced into making one mine, I'm just not feeling the draw.

'That's fabulous!' Aldo gasps, reaching for the same dress and checking the price tag. 'This is perfect for your date!'

Holding it against my body, Aldo pushes me towards a mirror and fluffs up my hair. Not being convinced, I shake my head and scrunch up my nose sceptically. 'It's a little over the top for a dinner...'

'You're meeting your future husband!' He scoffs, admiring the intricate needlework. '*Nothing* would be over the top!' Linking his arm through mine, Aldo holds the glittering dress in the air and leads me through the department store.

We have been shopping all day for the perfect outfit for my big date on Friday, but despite my best efforts to enjoy it, I just want to be at home.

'What about shoes?' Aldo stops in the aisle and points to a pair of pointed stilettoes. 'These are nice, or you could wear your Suave wedges? You still haven't worn those.'

I shrug my shoulders and glance at my watch. 'Either. I'm not too bothered...'

Not rising to the bait, he plucks the shoes from the display and drops them into his basket. 'Whether you show enthusiasm or not, you're going and that's final.'

Letting out a groan, I follow him towards the handbag section and nod in approval as he picks up a nude clutch bag. Listening to him ramble on about this season's must-have hairstyles, I zone out and allow myself to slip into a daydream. Nodding along in a bid to appear interested, I spin around as a certain name grabs my attention.

'... Surrey with Aidan...'

'Sorry?' I ask, suddenly on high alert. 'What was that?'

Rolling his eyes, Aldo tosses a necklace on top of the shoes before marching towards the tills. 'I *said*, I saw Pierce again whilst you were in Surrey with Aidan.'

'Oh.' I mumble, feeling deflated.

'He came into the salon.' Handing over the basket, Aldo motions for me to get my debit card out of my purse. 'He's really excited to meet you.'

I smile back at him as my stomach churns with dread. 'That's... *nice.*'

'Nice?' He repeats, shooting me a scowl. 'Believe me, Pierce Harrington is far more than *nice.*'

Secretly tiring of hearing this guy's name, I swap my card for the glossy bag and punch my PIN number into the keypad.

'I heard from Ruby a couple of days ago...' I mumble, trying to get away from the subject of Pierce. 'She's having a fabulous time out there.'

'I bet she is.' Aldo smiles and thanks the sales assistant. 'I'm glad she's finally living her dream.'

'What's *your* dream?' I ask, stuffing the receipt into the bag as we make our way towards the exit.

'I don't know.' He sighs and tears off his nicotine patch roughly. 'My dream changes day by day. One minute it's to own a salon in Chelsea, then it's to move to Mykonos...'

'Still in love with Greece?' I smile up at him and rest my head on his shoulder.

'Definitely.' Pulling an electronic cigarette from his pocket, he puffs away and blows smoke rings into the air. 'What about you?'

We step outside into the warm afternoon air and I automatically reach for my sunglasses. 'I've thought about this a lot lately and I've come to the conclusion that I'm already living my dream.'

'Really?' He asks, steering me in the direction of Blossom View.

'There are little things I would change here and there, but in the grand scheme of things, I would say I'm exactly where I want to be in life.' We join the line of people waiting to cross the road and I slip my hands into my pockets.

'I'm so proud of you, Shirley.' Aldo gives my shoulders a tight squeeze and pauses to look in a shop window. 'What made you come to that realisation?'

'I made an unhappiness list.' I glance up at him as he frowns in confusion. 'You write down all the things that make you unhappy and then you decide how you're going to change them. When I sat down to compose my list, I realised that my life is actually pretty good.'

'What was on the list?' He asks, slowing down to a steady pace and becoming absorbed in the conversation.

'It was pathetically short.' I admit, offering him a chewing gum. 'The first was to sort out the damp at Blossom View...'

'Oh, what problems you have!' He scoffs, nudging me playfully. 'What else was on the list?'

'To build bridges with my mum.' Knowing that Aldo is very aware of my fraught relationship with my mother, I bite my lip and wait for his reaction.

Stopping abruptly, Aldo's eyes widen in shock. 'Now *that* is something which needs sorting out.'

'It is.' I agree, grabbing his sleeve and pulling him along the street. 'We met up yesterday and I finally told her how she makes me feel. She cried, I cried and we agreed to start again.'

'Just like that? After all this time?' Aldo's jaw drops open and I nod to confirm what I am saying is true. 'I genuinely thought you two were a lost cause.'

'So did I.' I take a deep breath and look up through the trees. 'I'm not saying that all of our problems have suddenly vanished, but there's hope for us whilst we're both willing to try.'

'This is fantastic news!' Aldo pulls me towards him and hugs me tightly. 'You must be so happy.'

'I *am* happy.' I squeeze him back and feel a smile spring to my face. 'As long as I have hope, faith, a bed beneath me and the stars above me, all will be right with the world...'

*　*　*

Finally locating the tatty business card at the bottom of my handbag, I shake off the crumbs and turn it over in my hands. The corners are curled and it has a few grubby marks, but at least I haven't lost it. Running my eyes over the faded phone number, I walk over to the damp patch on the wall. Leaning down, I push against the skirting board and watch it crumble like sawdust beneath my touch. Hearing Aidan's words ringing loudly in my mind, I grab my phone and punch in the number in front of me.

The familiar ring buzzes for a few seconds before a deep voice picks up. Trying to explain that you think you have damp when you don't know what you're talking about is no easy feat and as a result, it takes me a while to arrange an appointment. Apparently, there are a hundred different types of damp and until he comes and sees it for himself, he won't know exactly what he's dealing with. Ending the call, I write a note on the fridge to remind me of the appointment and cross the last item off my unhappiness list.

Staring at the notepad, I feel a rush of satisfaction. The two things that have been worrying me are being taken care of. I finally feel in control. I feel like I have the power to change anything that I'm unhappy with and that's a whole new concept for me. Feeling rather pleased with myself, I bend down to pick up Mateo and head into the dining room.

After a quick lick of paint, courtesy of Aidan, the place looks twice the size it did before. It now looks fresh. It's a blank canvas for me to do whatever I please. Cradling my furry friend against my chest, I stand in the middle of the room and look around. This cottage will have once been filled with the laughter of so many people, but now it's time for me to make my own memories here. The past may have taught me a lot about myself, but this is where my future lies. Not in the Caribbean, not in New Zealand, but right here, in Blossom View. After all, home isn't a place, it's a feeling...

Chapter 36

For the first time in a long while, I awoke this morning feeling refreshed, rejuvenated and strangely content. I can't pinpoint exactly what has changed, but I have a funny feeling my blank unhappiness list has something to do with it. Taking a deep breath, I look around the room and smile happily. I'm ready and raring to go, some twenty minutes ahead of schedule. Deciding to use the spare time to re-stock the information stand, I look up as I hear the door squeak open.

'Yvette!' I exclaim, completely thrown to see her. 'You came!'

Looking at the circle of chairs nervously, she offers me a thin smile in response.

'It's great to see you.' Recognising her apprehension, I take a few steps towards her and motion for her to sit down. 'I'm so pleased that you decided to join us!'

'I haven't decided if I am staying yet.' She mumbles, clutching onto her handbag for dear life. 'I just wanted to see for myself what goes on in here.'

'That's absolutely fine.' Overjoyed that she has made the effort, I beam back at her proudly. 'There's no pressure. You just do as little or as much as you're comfortable with.'

Reluctantly nodding, she strains her neck to look at the educational posters on the wall.

'People won't be arriving for a little while. Feel free to have a look around.' Not wanting to pressure her, I return to the information stand and give her some space.

With wide eyes, she cautiously puts one foot in front of the other and joins me by the leaflets. Watching her pick up pamphlet after pamphlet, I inwardly give myself a high-five. Ruby would be overjoyed if she knew her mother was here.

'This will help Ruby so much...' I say encouragingly, reaching for a stack of contact cards and filling the empty container. 'Having the support of loved ones can have profound effects on sufferers of anxiety.'

Yvette nods and plucks another leaflet from the stand. Watching her quickly become engrossed in the text, I decide to leave her to it and walk into the lobby to give her a few minutes alone. Just making the decision to come here today was a giant step. I don't want to overload her with information too soon.

Sitting on the windowsill, I adjust the blinds to allow a little light to spill into the hallway and watch the flurry of people rushing along the street. The sun is dancing amongst the scattered clouds, as busy shoppers and workers go about their daily lives. Completely engrossed in the scene, I almost miss the shadowy figure walking across the car park. Pushing myself up, I frown at my watch as I see there are still ten minutes to go. Opening the door, my stomach flips as I see my own mother standing in front of me.

'Hi...' I stammer, blinking to make sure I'm not hallucinating. 'What are you doing here?'

Dusting a non-existent piece of fluff from her blazer, she purses her lips and looks behind me cautiously. 'I... I just thought it would be nice if I came along to see you in action.'

Completely floored by her presence, I stare back at her open-mouthed, totally lost for words.

Sensing my shock, her cheeks flush violently and she looks down at the ground in embarrassment. 'You mentioned that I didn't take an interest in your work and I wanted to show...'

'Thank you.' I whisper, cutting her off mid-sentence. 'I really appreciate it.'

Completely in awe that she actually took on board our conversation the other day, I stand frozen to the spot.

'So, can I come in?' She murmurs, smiling thinly.

Holding open the door, I beckon her inside and allow the door to close with a thud behind us. She's here. She has actually come along without being asked, pressured or begged to do so. Pinching myself discreetly, I wince as I realise I'm not dreaming.

Hearing the door open, Yvette looks over her shoulder as we step into the room.

'This is my mum.' I explain, hoping that the presence of another person doesn't scare her away. 'She's here for the same reason you are.'

'Hello.' Yvette says, in a matter of fact manner.

Holding out her hand for a polite shake, my mum nods sternly and the two of them stand in an uncomfortable silence. Looking at the scene in front of me, I move my gaze from Yvette to my mum and back again. Two mothers of two daughters, both of which have swallowed their pride, stopped making excuses and started to make an effort. It just goes to show that

no matter how far you've gone down the wrong road,
it's never too late to turn back and do the right thing...

Chapter 37

Staring at my reflection in the mirror, I lean towards the glass and try to recognise the woman staring back at me. For the past three hours, Aldo has preened and beautified me to perfection. My skin is flawless and my hair has been curled like it's never been curled before. I look like I'm getting ready to attend The Oscars, not a blind date that I have little to no interest in.

'I feel sick.' I groan nervously, as Aldo backcombs my hair into oblivion. 'I don't think I want to go.'

'That's a lie and you know it.' He retorts, grabbing a can of hairspray and fixing my tousled waves in place.

I manage a tiny smile and look down into my lap. He's right. Despite being incredibly nervous, I am intrigued to meet the famous Pierce Harrington. After how much Aldo has raved about him, I secretly can't wait to put a face to the name. I mean, is Aldo right? Has he really found my soulmate? Is Mr Harrington the man that I've been searching for all these years?

'You're all done.' He announces, standing back to admire his handiwork. 'Do you want a quick drink to calm your nerves?'

My stomach flips as he spritzes me with perfume. 'I already feel nauseous. I don't think throwing alcohol into the mix right now is a good idea.'

Aldo nods and grabs his car keys. 'Great, because there isn't time for one. Let's go.'

Following him outside, I hold on to his arm and cautiously hop into the car. As we pull away from Blossom View, my mouth becomes overwhelmingly dry as I realise just how nervous I am. This is my first date in over a year. A whole three hundred and sixty-five days have rolled by and I haven't had any kind of romantic involvement with a member of the male population.

Flipping down the visor, I peer into the mirror and give myself a silent pep talk. It's just dinner. A lovely lobster dinner with a man whom my best friend believes is my future husband. What better way is there to get back into the dating game?

'Do we need a code?' I ask suddenly, removing a tiny mascara smudge from beneath my left eye. 'Just in case I don't like him and need to make a swift escape?'

Aldo shakes his head and laughs. 'Trust me, you won't want to escape...'

We approach London Road and I try to calm my racing heart as I spot Il Migliore up ahead. The twinkling lights shine brightly against the sunset, creating the perfect backdrop for the perfect first date.

Closing my eyes to steady my breathing, I physically jump in my seat as Aldo pulls on the handbrake.

'What are you doing?' I scold, immediately tending to my ruffled curls.

'Jump out here. If we go around to the car park, you're going to be late.' Reaching across the seat, he gives me a quick hug as a car beeps behind us.

'But I just need a moment to compose myself...'
Trying to play for time, I take a deep breath as Aldo
ushers me out of the car.

'Just go! You will have an amazing time. I promise.'

With the irate driver becoming more enraged, I
push open the door and give Aldo a final wave.
Watching him drive away, I dither on the pavement
before making my way into the restaurant and
cautiously scanning the room. Is he already here? A
quick glance around the intimate dining area confirms
to me that he isn't. Not knowing whether that makes
this easier or more difficult, I give my name to the
waitress as she leads me to a quiet section of the
restaurant.

Taking a seat in a plush velvet chair, I order a glass
of fizz and admire the beautifully decorated booth.
The pristine cloth is adorned with dozens of tiny
crystals, each one soaking up the light from the
flickering candle in the centre of the table. If I could
design the perfect setting for the perfect date, this
would be it.

Suddenly feeling rather optimistic, I smile
gratefully as an ice-cold flute is discreetly placed in
front of me. Taking a much-needed sip, I get
comfortable in my seat and smooth down my dress.
It's exactly eight o'clock, which means he should be
here at any moment. Hearing footsteps heading my
way, I bite my lip as a tall figure comes to a stop at the
opposite side of the booth.

'Sadie?' A deep voice asks.

Forcing myself to look up, my lips stretch into a
smile as I take in the handsome man in front of me.

'Pierce Harrington...'

*   *   *

He's perfect. He's absolutely perfect. Aldo was
right. Pierce Harrington is more perfect than perfect
could possibly be. He's just... *faultless*. From his deep
chocolate eyes and head of dark curls, to his
impressive physique and infectious personality.
There's not a single thing about him that isn't
immaculate. He's well-educated, but not patronising
and passionate without being overbearing. Yes, Pierce
Harrington is most definitely a ten.

I honestly didn't believe men like this existed.
Pierce Harrington ticks all of the boxes and then
some. Every woman in the room is giving him the eye.
I can practically see love hearts floating around their
heads as they shamelessly admire my date. After my
disastrous last relationship, I would have been
perfectly happy meeting someone who simply wasn't
an adulterer or a commitment-phobe. Pierce has
certainly raised the bar in the dating game.

Thanking the waiter as he swaps my plate for a
delicious-looking dessert, I nod along as Pierce tells
me about his charity work for terminally ill children.
After many years as my best friend, Aldo clearly
knows exactly what I am looking for in a man. Pierce
and I have the same interests, we share the same
political views and we are both passionate about
matters of the mind. I have to hand it to him, Aldo has

found me absolutely everything I was searching for, all rolled into one devastatingly beautiful package.

Listening to him speak, I tell myself how lucky I am. My dream man is sitting right in front of me. I should be bouncing off the walls right now. I should be ecstatic at finally meeting such a wonderful guy, but something is missing. On paper, Pierce is flawless. He has absolutely everything that I thought I wanted, but something is missing. Regardless of how dreamy his eyes are, how lovely his smile is and how impeccable his manners are, that buzz inside me just isn't there. Of course, I am attracted to him, but is he a man I could envisage myself spending the rest of my life with?

Pierce's eyes soften as he talks about his gallery and I return his smile with a grin of my own. What is wrong with me? I am sat in a stunning restaurant, having a candlelit dinner with a fabulous man and I *still* feel as though there's a piece missing. Pierce is perfect. He's every woman's dream. If this isn't what I am looking for, what is? What is it I am holding out for?

Twirling my fingers around the stem of my glass, I study Pierce's handsome face and try to picture who I would rather have sat in his place. If Perfect Pierce isn't the one for me, who is? Where do you go to next when even perfect isn't good enough?

Resting my elbows on the table, I take a sip of bubbles and smile to myself. Maybe perfect isn't what I'm looking for after all. Perhaps perfect is overrated, because we weren't born to be perfect, we were born to be *real...*

Chapter 38

Passing the friendly builder a cup of tea, I stand back and watch him get to work. It turns out that the damp was much worse than he initially thought. If I wouldn't have taken Aidan's advice and addressed the issue, things would have quickly gone from bad to worse. As he strips back layer after layer of soggy plaster, I usher Mateo into the garden and take a seat on the bench.

After my date with Pierce last night, I had the rather awkward task of informing Aldo that I didn't want to see him again. Needless to say, that conversation went down like a lead balloon. As perfect as Pierce was, my heart was insistent that he wasn't the man for me. Throughout the course of the evening, I tried to ignore my gut instincts and convince myself otherwise, but the heart wants what it wants and bizarrely, my heart just doesn't want Pierce.

Pushing myself up, I follow Mateo between the rows of billowing laundry and come to a stop at the far end of the garden. Crouching down, I run my fingers through the dry ground and let out a surprised giggle. The seeds that Aldo and I planted have finally started to grow. Tiny green shoots are poking through the soil. They're barely visible, but the evidence is definitely there! New life is forming right before my eyes, but only now have I taken a moment to stop what I'm doing and appreciate it.

Looking over at Mateo, I smile to myself and lie back on the grass. Whether we realise it or not, there are new beginnings starting all around us, we're just too preoccupied with menial tasks to see them. Every time we open our eyes in the morning is another opportunity to rewrite the rules and change the direction in which our lives are going. Each day brings a new opportunity, a new adventure and a new chance to live life to the fullest. There are seven days in a week, but *someday* isn't one of them...

* * *

Staring at the blank canvas, I brush my hand over the fabric and sigh sadly. When I rolled out of bed this morning, I decided that today would be the day that I fell back in love with painting, but despite my many efforts to generate some enthusiasm, I just can't pick up a brush. With the builders busily working at the dreaded damp downstairs, Mateo and I are locked in the spare room, surrounded by paint, canvases and more brushes than I could ever dream to use.

Pulling over a stool, I bite my lip and force myself to pluck a brush from the pot. Hovering over a palette of rainbow-style colours, I dip the brush into a strip of forest green and hold it an inch from the easel. It's been so long since I dared to approach a canvas that I'm afraid of doing it wrong. Taking a deep breath, I brace myself before swiping the brush across the empty page. Relief washes over me as the canvas springs to life, making my shoulders feel instantly lighter. Laughing with joy, I dive back into the palette and add a splash of indigo to the mix.

My heart starts to race as one by one, I create a vibrant display of colour on the sheet in front of me. Adding smears of scarlet and splashes of sapphire breathes life back into a part of me that has been empty for so long. I failed to see it at the time, but when I wrote my unhappiness list, I missed one major thing and that was my artwork. Not having the passion to paint has clearly bothered me more than I realised. With each stroke of my brush I feel anxiety leaving my body. Every emotion that has built up inside me is being poured out onto the canvas and the result is stunning.

Art is my release. It is the place I come to when nothing else makes sense. I had become so obsessed with not returning to an easel until the time felt right, but in doing that I stopped appreciating the art that was all around me. Life itself is art. How we dress, the way we talk, how we smile and the way we laugh are all examples of the unique art we create without even realising it. Sometimes, that art doesn't turn out exactly as we would like, but the beauty is still there, you just have to try a little harder to see it.

Hearing a knock at the door, I abandon the colour palette and wipe my hands on my dungarees. With Mateo right behind me, I sprint down the stairs and quickly remove a blob of paint from my nose as I pull open the door. Feeling my jaw drop open, an astounded laugh escapes my lips.

'Aidan!' I exclaim, not being able to hide my joy. 'What are you doing here?'

Shrugging his shoulders, his eyes crease into a smile as he grins back at me. 'I asked myself that same question as I knocked on the door.'

I let out a shocked gasp as Mateo brushes past me to greet him. 'I... I thought you were going to New Zealand?'

'So did I...' Aidan brings his eyes up to meet mine and shakes his head. 'I got a cab to the airport, I had the tickets right there in my hand, but something inside me told me to tear them up.'

Reaching into his pocket, he produces a ticket that has been torn into a million pieces. Letting the shredded paper fall through his fingers like confetti, he takes a step towards me.

'Running away wasn't the answer. I need to put down roots and make my mark where I am happiest. Being in the airport made me realise that my future doesn't lie in New Zealand. My future is here, in Cheshire. I want to be surrounded by the countryside, I want to be close to the support group and most of all, I want to be close to you.'

Our eyes meet and I feel my heart pound in my chest as he picks up Mateo and nuzzles his nose against his.

'So, what do you say, Sadie Valentine? Can I come in?'

To be continued...

If you are struggling with anxiety, help is available to you.

Mind Infoline

0300 123 3393

Anxiety UK Infoline

08444 775 774

Anxiety United

www.anxietyunited.com

Follow Lacey London on Twitter

@thelaceylondon

Have you read the first book in the Anxiety Girl series?

Anxiety Girl

Sadie Valentine is just like you and I, or so she was...

Set in the glitzy and glamorous Cheshire village of Alderley Edge, Anxiety Girl is a story surrounding the struggles of a beautiful young lady who thought she had it all.

Once a normal-ish woman, mental illness wasn't something that Sadie really thought about, but when the three evils, anxiety, panic and depression creep into her life, Sadie wonders if she will ever see the light again.

With her best friend, Aldo, by her side, can Sadie crawl out of the impossibly dark hole and take back control of her life?

Once you have hit rock bottom, there's only one way to go...

Lacey London has spoken publicly about her own struggles with anxiety and hopes that Sadie will help other sufferers realise that there is light at the end of the tunnel.

The characters in this novel might be fictitious, but the feelings and emotions experienced are very real.

Meet Clara Andrews
Book 1

Meet Clara Andrews... Your new best friend!

With a love of cocktails and wine, a fantastic job in the fashion industry and the world's greatest best friends, Clara Andrews thought she had it all.

That is until a chance meeting introduces her to Oliver, a devastatingly handsome American designer. Trying to keep the focus on her work, Clara finds her heart stolen by Michelin starred restaurants and luxury hotels.

As things get flirty, Clara reminds herself that inter-office relationships are against the rules, so when a sudden recollection of a work's night out leads her to a cheeky, charming and downright gorgeous barman, she decides to see where it goes.

Clara soon finds out that dating two men isn't as easy as it seems...

Will she be able to play the field without getting played herself?

Join Clara as she finds herself landing in and out of trouble, re-affirming friendships, discovering truths and uncovering secrets.

Clara Meets the Parents
Book 2

Almost a year has passed since Clara found love in the arms of delectable American Oliver Morgan and things are starting to heat up.

The nights of tequila shots and bodycon dresses are now a distant memory, but a content Clara couldn't be happier about it.

It's not just Clara things have changed for. Marc is settling in to his new role as Baby Daddy and Lianna is lost in the arms of the hunky Dan once again.

When Oliver declares it time to meet the Texan in-laws, Clara is ecstatic and even more so when she discovers that the introduction will take place on the sandy beaches of Mexico!

Will Clara be able to win over Oliver's audacious mother?

What secrets will unfold when she finds an ally in the beautiful and captivating Erica?

Clara is going to need a little more than sun, sand and margaritas to get through this one...

Meet Clara Morgan
Book 3

When Clara, Lianna and Gina all find themselves engaged at the same time, it soon becomes clear that things are going to get a little crazy.

With Lianna and Gina busy planning their own impending nuptials, it's not long before Oliver enlists the help of Janie, his feisty Texan mother, to help Clara plan the wedding of her dreams.

However, it's not long before Clara realizes that Janie's vision of the perfect wedding day is more than a little different to her own.

Will Clara be able to cope with her shameless mother-in-law Janie?

What will happen when a groom gets cold feet?

And how will Clara handle a blast from the past who makes a reappearance in the most unexpected way possible?

Join Clara and the gang as three very different brides, plan three very different weddings.

With each one looking for the perfect fairy tale ending, who will get their happily ever after...

Clara at Christmas
Book 4

With snowflakes falling and fairy lights twinkling brightly, it can only mean one thing - Christmas will be very soon upon us.

With just twenty-five days to go until the big day, Clara finds herself dealing with more than just the usual festive stresses.

Plans to host the perfect Christmas Day for her American in-laws are ambushed by her BFF's clichéd meltdown at turning thirty.

With a best friend on the verge of a mid-life crisis, putting Christmas dinner on the table isn't the only thing Clara has got to worry about this year.

Taking on the role of Best Friend/Therapist, Head Chef and Party Planner is much harder than Clara had anticipated.

With the clock ticking, can Clara pull things together - or will Christmas Day turn out to be the December disaster that she is so desperate to avoid?

Join Clara and the gang in this festive instalment and discover what life changing gifts are waiting for them under the tree this year...

Meet Baby Morgan
Book 5

It's fair to say that pregnancy hasn't been the joyous journey that Clara had anticipated. Extreme morning sickness, swollen ankles and crude cravings have plagued her for months and now that she has gone over her due date, she is desperate to get this baby out of her.

With a lovely new home in the leafy, affluent village of Spring Oak, Clara and Oliver are ready to start this new chapter in their lives. The cot has been bought, the nursery has been decorated and a name has been chosen. All that is missing, is the baby himself.

As Lianna is enjoying new found success with her interior design firm, Periwinkle, Clara turns to the women of the village for company. The once inseparable duo find themselves at different points in their lives and for the first time in their friendship, the cracks start to show.

Will motherhood turn out to be everything that Clara ever dreamed of?

Which naughty neighbour has a sizzling secret that she so desperately wants to keep hidden?

Laugh, smile and cry with Clara as she embarks on her journey to motherhood. A journey that has some unexpected bumps along the way. Bumps that she never expected...

Clara in the Caribbean
Book 6

Almost a year has passed since Clara returned to the big smoke and she couldn't be happier to be back in her city.

With the perfect husband, her best friends for neighbours and a beautiful baby boy, Clara feels like every aspect of her life has finally fallen into place.

It's not just Clara who things are going well for. The Strokers have made the move back from the land down under and Lianna is on cloud nine – literally.

Not only has she been jetting across the globe with her interior design firm, Periwinkle, she has also met the man of her dreams... again.

For the past twelve months Li has been having a long distance relationship with Vernon Clarke, a handsome man she met a year earlier on the beautiful island of Barbados.

After spending just seven short days together, Lianna decided that Vernon was the man for her and they have been Skype smooching ever since.

Due to Li's disastrous dating history, it's fair to say that Clara is more than a little dubious about Vernon being 'The One.' So, when her neighbours invite Clara to their villa in the Caribbean, she can't resist the chance of checking out the mysterious Vernon for herself.

Has Lianna finally found true love?

Will Vernon turn out to a knight in shining armour or just another fool in tin foil?

Grab a rum punch and join Clara and the gang as they fly off to paradise in this sizzling summer read!

Clara in America
Book 7

With Clara struggling to find the perfect present for her baby boy's second birthday, she is pleasantly surprised when her crazy mother-in-law, Janie, sends them tickets to Orlando.

After a horrendous flight, a mix-up at the airport and a let-down with the weather, Clara begins to question her decision to fly out to America.

Despite the initial setbacks, the excitement of Orlando gets a hold of them and the Morgans start to enjoy the fabulous Sunshine State.

Too busy having fun in the Florida sun, Clara tries to ignore the nagging feeling that something isn't quite right.

Does Janie's impromptu act of kindness have a hidden agenda?

Just as things start to look up, Janie drops a bombshell that none of them saw coming.

Can Clara stop Janie from making a huge mistake, or has Oliver's audacious mother finally gone too far?

Join Clara as she gets swept up in a world of fast food, sunshine and roller coasters.

With Janie refusing to play by the rules, it looks like the Morgans are in for a bumpy ride...

Clara in the Middle
Book 8

It's been six months since Clara's crazy mother-in-law took up residence in the Morgan's spare bedroom and things are starting to get strained.

Between bringing booty calls back to the apartment and teaching Noah curse words, Janie's outrageous behaviour has become worse than ever.

When she agreed to this temporary arrangement, Clara knew it was only a matter of time before there were fireworks. But with Oliver seemingly oblivious to Janie's shocking actions, Clara feels like she has nowhere to turn.

Thankfully for Clara, she has a fluffy new puppy and a job at her friend's lavish florist to take her mind off the problems at home.

Throwing herself into her work, Clara finds herself feeling extremely grateful for her great circle of friends, but when one of them puts her in an incredibly awkward situation she starts to feel more alone than ever.

Will Janie's risky behaviour finally push a wedge between Clara and Oliver?

How will Clara handle things when Eve asks her for the biggest favour you could ever ask?

With Clara feeling like she is stuck in the middle of so many sticky situations, will she be able to keep everybody happy?

Join Clara and the gang as they tackle more family dramas, laugh until they cry and test their friendships to the absolute limit.

Clara's Last Christmas
Book 9

Just a few months ago, life seemed pretty rosy indeed. With Lianna back in London for good, Clara had been enjoying every second with her best friend.

From blinged-up baby shopping with Eve to wedding planning with a delirious Dawn, Clara and her friends were happier than ever.

Unfortunately, their happiness is short lived, as just weeks before Christmas, Oliver and Marc discover that their jobs are in jeopardy.

With Clara helping Eve to prepare for not one, but two new arrivals, news that Suave is going into administration rocks her to the core.

It may be December, but the prospect of being jobless at Christmas means that not everyone is feeling festive. Do they give up on Suave and move on, or can the gang work as one to rescue the company that brought them all together?

Can Clara and her friends save Suave in time for Christmas?

Made in the USA
Middletown, DE
13 November 2018